MW01491714

FICTION

NON-FICTION

Neil Clarke: Publisher/Editor-in-Chief
Sean Wallace: Editor
Kate Baker: Non-Fiction Editor/Podcast Director
Gardner Dozois: Reprint Editor

Clarkesworld Magazine (ISSN: 1937-7843) • Issue 89 • February 2014

Tortoiseshell Cats Are Not Refundable

CAT RAMBO

Antony bought the kit at Fry's in the gray three months after Mindy's death. He swam in and out of fog those days, but he still went frequently to the electronics store and drifted through its aisles, examining hard drives, routers, televisions, microphones, video games, garden lights, refrigerators, ice cream makers, rice cookers, all with the same degree of interest. Which was to say little to none, barely a twitch on the meter. A jump of the arrow from E up to one.

A way to kill time. So were the evenings, watching reality shows and working his way methodically through a few joints. If pot hadn't been legal in Seattle, it would've been booze, he knew, but instead the long, hard, lonely evening hours were a haze of blue smoke until he finally found himself nodding off and hauled himself into bed for a few hours of precious oblivion.

He prized those periods of nothingness.

Each day began with that horrible moment when he put a hand out to touch Mindy's shoulder—hey, honey, I had this awful dream you died, in a boating accident, no less, when was last time we were on a *boat*. Then the stomach dropping realization, sudden as stepping out into an elevator shaft.

Not.

A.

Dream.

His mother called him every day at first, but he couldn't manage the responses. Let alone the conversational give and take.

That saddened him. Made him feel guilty too. He was the only child his mother still had nearby. Both of his sisters had stayed on the other coast and were distant now as then. Still angry at his mother for

1

unimaginable transgressions during their high school years. They both had been excellent at holding a grudge all their lives. He was the only child who'd been willing to take some responsibility for her, had helped her move out to this coast in fact.

He loved her. Bought her presents. That was how the cat, a small tortoiseshell kitten, had entered her life, riding in his coat pocket, a clot of black and orange fur, tiny triangular face split between the colors.

His mother had named it, as with all her animals, palindromically. Taco Cat, like God Dog and Dribybird the parakeet.

She loved that cat about as much as she'd ever loved anything. His mother had always been stolid and self-contained, but he knew she missed the cat even now, a year after its death.

She deserved something to fill her days. He wondered if they'd been as gray as his were nowadays, ever since his father died. He thought—hoped, perhaps—that wasn't true.

Maybe you did get over it with time.

He read somewhere that older people did better, were happier, if they had something they could care for. Taco had been that and now that prop was gone.

He'd replace it.

The kit was one of those late-night things. Infomercial fodder. Clone a beloved pet. Take the sample and send it into their labs. Have a perfect replica delivered within three months. A box 500 times larger than it needed to be, holding only the test tube in which you would put the fragments of hair or claw material that were required.

He teased clumps from the wire brush he'd taken from his mother's, poked it with a forefinger into the test tube's depths. Stoppered it with a blunt plastic round.

Used his shunt to scan in the bar code on its side and beam it to the mailing center. A drone pecked at his apartment window, three floors up. Colored UPS brown. He could see other brightly colored shipping drones, colored red and green for the holidays, zipping around closer to the street. He authenticated it, staring into its inquisitive eye, and received the confirmation number displayed to one side, hovering in the air before it disappeared.

He was part of the last generation to know what life was like without a shunt. He got one in college, finally, had sold all the gold coins his aunt Mick, who died in the seventh Gulf War, had left him, and he never regretted that.

Life was so much more reliable with the shunt. It made sure you didn't overeat by making you feel satiated after just a few mouthfuls or let you sleep as long and deep as you liked, and even take part in preprogrammed dreams. You could use it to upload knowledge packs, particularly if you had augmented memory. It let you remember everyone's face and every date and time you ever needed to. It was like minor superpowers.

How awesome to live inside the future. Or it should have been.

He'd never thought much about his existence before Mindy. Then all of a sudden he *wanted* a life, a life together full of jokes only they shared. Him cooking her ginger pancakes and spending Sunday mornings lazing in shunt-enhanced sex, pleasurable and languorous and amazing.

He was leaving after a dinner of enchiladas unsatisfyingly sauced, their edges crisp and brown, stabbing the mouth. His mother hadn't mentioned Mindy outright, but she patted him on the upper arm as he paused to slip on his jacket. The gesture was unusual, outside her usual air-kiss intimacies.

He said, "Do you have Taco's old brush?"

"In the cupboard."

It shook him to see all the cat's things, gathered in careful memorial. He didn't associate sentimentality with his mother. Loss did that to you, perhaps. Though she'd endured his father's loss without such a display. At least he thought so. He tried to think back to his father's death. How long had it taken her to send all those shirts and ties and suits to St. Vincent De Paul's thrift shop? Not long. He remembered railing at her angrily about it. He'd planned on wearing all those clothes, two sizes too big for his 16 year old frame, some day.

"It doesn't pay to get attached," she'd said. Her dry eyes infuriated him even farther. She'd hugged her arms to herself and returned his angry stare.

He still had things to make up to her for. This would help even the scales so tipped by all his adolescent anger and outbreaks.

BCSS sent him an envelope. The language of the thick packet was dense: an opportunity extended him to participate in a test program.

Clone a human.

Give him Mindy back.

He said, "I don't understand how it's possible. I know you can replicate her body, but her mind?"

Dr. Avosh's eyes were clearly artificial, flat circles of emerald green. What did it say about her, that she didn't even bother to try to hide her augmentations?

She said, "We create a matrix of artificial memories. Easy nowadays."

"But where do those memories come from?"

"We have more material than you would think. Social media, public records, and some information garnered from the shunt itself."

That startled him. "Shunts don't record things." There had been plenty of legal battles over that.

"No," Dr. Avosh said. "That's a misconception most people share. While the original versions only recorded what you wanted them to, and had limited memory space, the current versions record a great deal. It's simply inadmissible in court." One of her pupils was markedly larger than the other. As he looked at it, it ratcheted even further wide.

"Are you recording this right now?" he asked.

"It's my policy to record everything."

"In case you ever need to be replicated."

She shook her head, then hesitated. "Not really. There are so many reasons to do so."

"Are they real memories?"

"Are you asking if they are detailed memories? No. More like a memory of a memory, and obviously there will be gaps. It won't be quite the same for you, but for her it will be much smoother. She'll believe herself to be the actual Mindy. We recommend you not talk to her about the actual circumstances until at least six months have passed."

Mindy. The smell of her hair when he buried his nose in it, inhaling the scent as delicious as cinnamon or roses, a musky edge that always tugged at the edges of his erotic conscious.

There was no way he could say no.

"You said this was a new process. How many times has it been done?"

"This is the third trial batch of subjects. The first time we're using people in your situation."

"My situation?"

Papers on her desk whispered against each other as she fiddled with them. "Recently bereaved. We're curious to see how much the spouse's memory can augment the process and reinforce beliefs."

She paused. "And I must tell you that the company doesn't cover the entire cost."

He'd met Mindy on the R train, heading from his Bay Ridge apartment up into Manhattan to work for the BWSS. He'd handled their computer systems, going in late at night to work through the morning hours maintaining the message boards the BWSS scientists used.

You saw the same people on the train sometimes. He'd noticed her right away: small and birdlike. Always smiling, in a way you didn't hit in NYC. Curious and unafraid, chatting with the woman beside her one day, looking at kid pictures, the next day helping an old man to a seat.

That was Mindy. Friendly. Finally one day she plopped down beside him and said, "Here we go!"

Why she'd said it, she didn't know, she told him later, but indeed they went, first chatting daily, then going for coffee and then with perfect amity, dating, engagement, marriage in a small chapel attended only by close friends and family.

She had so many friends and they seemed to welcome him into the circle, saying, "Take care of her!"

He had. Until the accident.

Now every day that dizzying fall into the realization she wasn't there.

Any price was worth paying to avoid that.

But costly, so costly. He'd plundered his 401(k), his IRAs, taken out a second mortgage. Cut his bills to the bone and still had to ask his mother for money.

She provided it without question once she found out what it was for.

They drew as much as they could on his memories, which meant going in every day for two weeks in a row, sitting there talking about his relationship with Mindy, his history, where they'd gone on their honeymoon, and what a typical trip to the grocery store was like, and where each piece of their bedroom furniture had come from. Dr. Avosh said that was good. The stronger the relationship with him was, the more quickly the cloned Mindy would adjust.

His mother didn't ask about the results or the loan she'd made him to pay for the process. He thought perhaps she was trying to keep him from getting his hopes up too far, but as he aged, increasingly he realized he didn't understand his mother, didn't understand the parts of her that she had kept closed away from her family. It was only in his 40s that they had become something like close.

Instead, they talked about the day-to-day drama of her apartment building. He grew interested despite himself, even though the stories were so small, concerning misplaced mail or who shoveled the front walk.

He said, "I got you a present. It should arrive next week. According to the tracking number it's being prepared for shipment right now."

"Should I ask what it is?"

He found himself smiling and the expression almost startled him. How long had it been since the gray had lifted momentarily? Too long.

He and Mindy would laugh about that together eventually. He wondered what that would be like, to be able to say, "While you were dead."

Perhaps it would be better just not to bring that up. He couldn't even begin to imagine what it would be like to live on the other side of that.

"Your present arrived," his mother said. "It's very nice." Her voice was strained.

"You don't like it?" he said.

"Of course I do," she said, but he could tell she was lying.

When he went for dinner, he realized the problem.

"They must have shipped you the wrong cat," he said, looking down at it. It was the same size as Taco and it was a tortoiseshell, but where Taco had been black with dapplings of hazy orange hair, this one was white with awkward splotches of orange and brown.

But the service rep explained. "You can't clone tortoiseshells and expect the same markings. They're random expressions of the gene. The brochure lists certain animals where you can't get an exact copy. Tortoiseshell cats are not refundable."

He hung up abruptly, full of rage. For God's sake, he couldn't get anything right lately.

But that would change when Mindy was back.

He didn't see the new cat the next time he was over and he didn't ask questions.

He could understand loving one configuration but not another.

But he didn't want to think about that.

They sent a crew that went over the house, scanning in everything about it. They quizzed him about the usual state of cleanliness, and what days Mindy usually cleaned on, what she was good at and what she was bad at, and how much they actually split up the chores. Her favorite brands.

He didn't know many of the answers. How empty did the refrigerator have to get before she'd go shopping, since she was the one who handled all that? He had no idea. They took another tack and asked him what he remembered them running out of, milk or toilet paper or butter.

"You see, most people have a few trigger items that automatically send them to the store," the data technician chirped at him as she continued running her bar scanner over everything under the sink. She'd quizzed him as to what he purchased and what Mindy had and luckily his only contribution had been a bottle of lime-scented dishwashing soap.

"Have you done many of these before?" he asked.

Her fingers kept clicking over the data pad. She had long thin nails with tiny daggers painted in silver at each tip and a tiny border of circles. "Two so far."

"What were they like?"

"The first preferred Comet and Pine-Sol, the second went with Seventh Generation cleaning products."

"No. I meant . . . " He wasn't sure how to formulate it. "Did it, did it work?"

Her gaze was quizzical. "All I can tell you is that, sure, when they came back they liked the same cleaning brands." She clicked and swiped. "All right, new section. Bed, made or unmade on a regular basis? If the former, who did it?"

"We did it together every morning," he said. His eyes heated up and he hoped he wasn't getting too teary. She tapped away.

"You two were sweet. It will be just as cute in the next round. You'll see."

He brought himself to ask his mother what she'd done with the cat. Her hands faltered as she chopped onions, then resumed their staccato beat.

"Ms. Green two doors down had mice," she said. "So I loaned her Taco Two."

"Taco Two? No palindrome?" he asked.

A sizzle and then a wave of fragrance as she added the onions to the skillet. "I couldn't think of one yet. I'm sure it'll come to me eventually."

"Eventually," he repeated agreeably. He thought perhaps the cat would end up staying with Mrs. Green, but that was all right.

"So what else is new?"

"I'm bringing her home tomorrow."

She put the spatula down in order to swing around and look at him, wide-eyed. "So soon?"

He nodded. He was smiling again. She smiled back, wiping her hands on her apron before she came over to awkwardly hug him.

What do you bring to your first meeting with the person you used to be married to? He chose an armload of roses. Who cared if it was cliché? Mindy loved them.

He remembered buying them for her. The two of them together at the farmers market, wandering from stall to stall, buying bread rounds still warm from baking and bags of vegetables still thick with dirt and leaves.

The way she managed to look at every display, ferreted out everything interesting, made people smile as she talked to them.

Roses. So much like her in the way she opened to the world.

Glimpsed through the pane of glass in the door, she seemed so small in the hospital bed. Her eyes were shut. Her hair had once been long, but now it was short, one or two inches at most.

He said to Dr. Avosh. "Why did you cut her hair?"

The doctor chuckled. "I can see where it would seem that way. But it's because we've had a limited amount of time for her to grow hair in. It'll come."

"Won't that mess with her memories?"

"We've compensated." The doctor put her hand on the gray metal doorknob before looking back over her shoulder at him. "Are you ready to say hello?"

He nodded, unable to speak around the lump in his throat.

The room smelled of lemon disinfectant. The nurse already there took the flowers from him with a muted squeal of delight. "Aren't these pretty! I'll put them in water."

Mindy's eyes were still shut.

"Are you awake, Mindy?" the doctor said. "You have a visitor."

Her eyes opened, fixing on him immediately. "Antony."

The same smile, the same voice.

Emotion pushed him to the bed and he gathered her hands in his, kissing them over and over, before he laid his head down on the cool white hospital sheet and cried for the first time since she died.

He'd asked before what sort of cover story they would have for her waking up in the hospital. Of course they'd thought of that already: a slip in the shower, a knock on the head that accounted for any dizziness or disorientation.

He'd prepared the house as well, made it as close as he could remember to their days together, removed the dingy detritus of a bachelor existence by bringing a cleaning service in. If it seemed too different and she questioned it, he'd tell her that he'd hired the service to help him cope while she was in the hospital.

In the taxi home, as they rumbled their way up Queen Anne, he noticed it.

She didn't look at the world in the same way anymore. A shrinking back, a momentary flinch, a hesitancy about it all.

He asked the doctor about it the next day. He could tell from her expression that she knew the answer already, but was reluctant to say. He pushed harder. "Does it mean something went wrong with the process?"

"Of course not," Dr. Avosh snapped. She shook her head. "We still don't understand all the ways that personality is genetically determined."

"If it's genetically determined, then it would be the same," he said.

"It's considerably more complicated than that," she said and began to explain, but he was already thinking of tortoiseshell cats and realizing what he had done.

He couldn't think of anywhere to go but his mother's.

Much to his surprise, she was sitting on the sofa with Taco on her lap.

"I thought you gave her to Mrs. Green," he said.

She ran her hand over the soft fur, rubbing around the base of the cat's ears. He could hear it purring from where he sat. "Just a loan," she said. "Shall I make us some coffee?"

They sat together, drinking it. The cat hopped back onto his mother's lap and began to purr again. She patted it.

"She's more loving, this time around," she said.

"This time around?"

"Yes." She shrugged and kept petting the cat.

"I think Mindy is different this time around too," he said.

She looked up, brows furrowed. "Is it possible?"

He nodded at the cat in her lap. "It's the same thing, as far as I can tell. Personality is random, at least some of it."

"But she looks just the same."

He rubbed his forehead with the heel of his hand. "Yes, she does. They took great care in that regard. I wouldn't be surprised if they used plastic surgery to correct any discrepancies. But they can't do that with her personality."

"And you can't tell her."

He shook his head.

His mother smoothed her hand over the cat, whispered to it.

"What's that?" he said.

"Asking her what she makes of this."

"But you called her something."

She blushed. "Taco Tooto Cat. Not Taco, but Taco Too."

Not and yet and still.

Like his Mindy. Who he could finally grieve for. Who he could finally meet for the first time.

"Are you going to pretend?" his mother said.

"No," he said. "I'm going to tell her. And tell her why she feels about me like she does. Then she can decide."

9

"Decide whether or not to keep things as they were?"
"No. Decide whether or not to begin."

ABOUT THE AUTHOR

Cat Rambo lives, writes, and teaches by the shores of an eagle-haunted lake in the Pacific Northwest. Her fiction publications include stories in *Asimov's, Clarkesworld Magazine,* and *Tor.com.* Her short story, "Five Ways to Fall in Love on Planet Porcelain," from story collection *Near + Far* (Hydra House Books), was a 2012 Nebula nominee. Her editorship of *Fantasy Magazine* earned her a World Fantasy Award nomination in 2012.

The Eleven Holy Numbers of the Mechanical Soul

NATALIA THEODORIDOU

a=38. This is the first holy number.

Stand still. Still. In the water. Barely breathing, spear in hand. One with the hand.

A light brush against my right calf. The cold and glistening touch of human skin that is not human. Yet, it's something. Now strike. Strike.

Theo had been standing in the sea for hours—his bright green jacket tied high around his waist, the water up to his crotch. Daylight was running out. The fish was just under the point of his spear when he caught a glimpse of a beast walking towards him. Animalis Primus. The water was already lapping at its first knees.

He struck, skewering the middle of the fish through and through. It was large and cumbersome—enough for a couple of days. It fought as he pulled it out of the water. He looked at it, its smooth skin, its pink, human-like flesh. These fish were the closest thing to a human being he'd seen since he crashed on Oceanus.

Theo's vision blurred for a moment, and he almost lost his balance. The fish kept fighting, flapping against the spear.

It gasped for air.

He drove his knife through its head and started wading ashore.

Animalis Primus was taking slow, persistent steps into the water. Its stomach bottles were already starting to fill up, its feet were tangled in seaweed. Soon, it would drown.

Theo put the fish in the net on his back and sheathed his spear to free both his hands. He would need all of his strength to get the beast back on the beach. Its hollow skeleton was light when dry, but wet, and with the sea swelling at dusk—it could take them both down.

When he got close enough, Theo placed his hands against the hips of the advancing beast to stop its motion, then grabbed it firmly by its horizontal spine to start pushing it in the other direction. The beast moved, reluctantly at first, then faster as its second knees emerged from the water and met less resistance. Finally its feet gained traction against the sand, and soon Theo was lying on his back, panting, the fish on one side, the beast on the other, dripping on the beach and motionless. But he was losing the light. In a few moments, it would be night and he would have to find his way back in the dark.

He struggled to his feet and stood next to the beast.

"What were you doing, mate?" he asked it. "You would have drowned if I hadn't caught you, you know that?"

He knelt by the beast's stomach and examined the bottles. They were meant to store pressurized air—now they were full of water. Theo shook his head. "We need to empty all these, dry them. It will take some time." He looked for the tubing that was supposed to steer the animal in the opposite direction when it came in contact with water. It was nowhere to be found.

"All right," he said. "We'll get you fixed soon. Now let's go home for the night, ja?"

He threw the net and fish over his shoulder and started pushing Animalis Primus towards the fuselage.

b=41,5. This is the second holy number.

Every night, remember to count all the things that do not belong here. So you don't forget. Come on, I'll help you.

Humans don't belong here. Remember how you couldn't even eat the fish at first, because they reminded you too much of people, with their sleek skin, their soft, scaleless flesh? Not any more, though, ja? I told you, you would get over it. In time.

Animals don't belong here, except the ones we make.

Insects.

Birds.

Trees. Never knew I could miss trees so much.

Remember how the fish gasped for air? Like I would. Like I am.

It will be light again in a few hours. Get some sleep, friend. Get some sleep.

• • •

The wind was strong in the morning. Theo emerged from the fuselage and tied his long gray hair with an elastic band. It was a good thing he'd tethered Animalis Primus to the craft the night before.

He rubbed his palms together over the dying fire. There was a new sore on the back of his right hand. He would have to clean it with some saltwater later. But there were more important things to do first.

He walked over to the compartment of the craft that he used as a storage room and pulled free some white tubing to replace the damaged beast's water detector. He had to work fast. The days on Oceanus waited for no man.

About six hours later, the bottles in Animalis Primus were empty and dry, a new binary step counter and water detector installed. All he had to do now was test it.

Theo pushed the beast towards the water, its crab-like feet drawing helixes in the wet sand. He let the beast walk to the sea on its own. As soon as the detector touched the surf, Animalis Primus changed direction and walked away from the water.

Theo clapped. "There you go, mate!" he shouted. "There you go!"

The beast continued to walk, all clank and mechanical grace. As it passed by Theo, it stopped, as if hesitating.

Then, the wind blew, and the beast walked away.

Dusk again, and the winds grew stronger. Nine hours of day, nine hours of night. Life passed quickly on Oceanus.

Theo was sitting by the fire just outside the fuselage. He dined on the rest of the fish, wrapped in seaweed. Seaweed was good for him, good source of vitamin C, invaluable after what was left of the craft's supplies ran out, a long time ago. He hated the taste, though.

He looked at the beasts, silhouetted against the night sky and the endless shore:

Animalis Acutus, walking sideways with its long nose pointed at the wind,

Animalis Agrestis, the wild, moving faster than all of them combined,

Animalis Caecus, the blind, named irrationally one night, in a bout of despair,

Animalis Echinatus, the spiny one, the tallest,

Animalis Elegans, the most beautiful yet, its long white wings undulating in the wind with a slight, silky whoosh,

and Animalis Primus, now about eight years old, by a clumsy calculation. The oldest one still alive.

Eight years was not bad. Eight years of living here were long enough to live.

c=39,3. This is the third holy number.

Now listen, these beasts, they are simple Jansen mechanisms with a five-bar linkage at their core. Mechanical linkages are what brought about the Industrial Revolution, ja? I remember reading about them in my Archaic Mechanics studies.

See, these animals are all legs, made of those electrical tubes we use to hide wires in. Each leg consists of a pair of kite-like constructions that are linked via a hip and a simple crank. Each kite is made up of a pentagon and a triangle, the apex of which is the beast's foot. The movement is created by the relative lengths of the struts. That's why the holy numbers are so important. They are what allows the beasts to walk. To live.

Each beast needs at least three pairs of legs to stand by itself, each leg with its very own rotary motion. All the hips and cranks are connected via a central rod. That's the beast's spine.

And then, of course, there are the wings. The wind moves the wings, and the beasts walk on their own.

They have wings, but don't fool yourself into thinking they can fly, ja? Wings are not all it takes to fly.

In the morning, Theo was so weak he could barely use the desalination pump to get a drink of water and wash his face. He munched on seaweed, filling up on nutrients, trying to ignore the taste. After all these years, he had still not gotten used to that taste. Like eating rot right off of the ocean bed.

The beasts were herding by the nearest sand dune today, mostly immobilized by the low wind. The sun shone overhead, grinding down Theo's bones, the vast stretches of sand and kelp around him. The beach. His beach.

He had walked as far from the sea as he could, the first months on Oceanus. All he had found was another shore on the other side of this swath of land. All there was here was this beach. All there was, this ocean.

He poured some saltwater on the new wounds on his knees. The pain radiated upwards, like a wave taking over his body.

The winds suddenly grew stronger. There was the distant roar of thunder.

Theo let himself be filled by the sound of the sand shifting under the force of the wind, by the sound of the rising waves, by this ocean that was everything. The ocean filled him up, and the whole world fell away, and then Theo fell away and dissolved, and life was dismantled, and only the numbers were left.

a=38 b=41,5 c=39,3 d=40,1 e=55,8 f=39,4 g=36,7 h=65,7 i=49 j=50 k=61,9 a=38 b=41,5 c=39,3 d=40,1 e=55,8 f=39,4 g=36,7 h=65,7 i=49 j=50 k=61,9 a=38 b=41,5 c=39,3 d=40,1 e=55,8 f=39,4 g=36,7 h=65,7 i=49 j=50 k=61,9 a=38 b=41,5 c=39,3 d=40,1 e=55,8 f=39,4 g=36,7 h=65,7 i=49 j=50 k=61,9 a=38 b=41,5 c=39,3 d=40,1 e=55,8 f=39,4 g=36,7 h=65,7 i=49 j=50 k=61,9 a=38 b=41,5 c=39,3 d=40,1 e=55,8 f=39,4 g=36,7 h=65,7 i=49 j=50 k=61,9 a=38 b=41,5 c=39,3 d=40,1 e=55,8 . . .

At night, like every night, Theo sent messages to the stars. Sometimes he used the broken transmitter from the craft; others, he talked to them directly, face to face.

"Stars," he said, "are you lonely? Are you there, stars?"

d=40,1. This is the fourth holy number.

You know, at first I thought this was a young planet. I thought that there was so little here because life was only just beginning. I could still study it, make all this worthwhile. But then, after a while, it became clear. The scarcity of lifeforms. The powdery sand, the absence of seashells, the traces of radiation, the shortage of fish. The fish, the improbable fish. It's obvious, isn't it? We are closer to an end than we are to a beginning. This ecosystem has died. We, here; well. We are just the aftermath.

Stars, are you there?

Day again, and a walk behind the craft to where his companions were buried. Theo untangled the kelp that had been caught on the three steel rods marking their graves, rearranged his red scarf around Tessa's rod. Not red any more—bleached and worn thin from the wind and the sun and the rain.

"It was all for nothing, you know," he said. "There is nothing to learn here. This place could never be a home for us."

He heard a beast approaching steadily, its cranks turning, its feet landing rhythmically on the sand. It was Animalis Primus. A few more steps and it would tread all over the graves. Theo felt blood rush to his head. He started waving his hands, trying to shoo the beast, even though he knew better. The beast did not know grave. All it knew was water and not-water.

"Go away!" he screamed. "What do you want, you stupid piece of trash?" He ran towards the beast and pushed it away, trying to make it move in the opposite direction. He kicked loose one of its knees. Immediately, the beast stopped moving.

Theo knelt by the beast and hid his face in his palms. "I'm sorry," he whispered. "I'm so sorry."

A slight breeze later, the beast started to limp away from the graves, towards the rest of its herd.

Theo climbed to his feet and took a last look at his companions' graves.

"We died for nothing," he said, and walked away.

At night, Theo made his fire away from the craft. He lay down, with his back resting on a bed of dry kelp, and took in the night, the darkness, the clear sky.

He imagined birds flying overhead.

Remember birds?

e=55,8. This is the fifth holy number.

A few years ago the sea spit out the carcass of a bird. I think it was a bird. I pulled it out of the water, all bones and feathers and loose skin. I looked at it and looked at it, but I couldn't understand it. Where had it come from? Was it a sign of some sort? Perhaps I was supposed to read it in some way? I pulled it apart using my hands, looked for the fleshy crank that used to animate it. I found nothing. I left it there on the sand. The next morning it was gone.

Did you imagine it?

Perhaps I imagined it. Or maybe this planet is full of carcasses, they just haven't found me yet.

How do you know it was a bird?

Have you ever seen birds?

Are you sure?

Theo's emaciated body ached as he pulled himself up from the cold sand. He shouldn't sleep outside, he knew that much.

How much of this sand is made of bone?

Had the winds come during the night, he could have been buried under a dune in a matter of minutes. Animalis Elegans was swinging its wings in the soft breeze, walking past him, when a brilliant flash of light bloomed in the sky. A comet. It happened, sometimes.

Are you there? he thought.

Are you lonely?

f=39,4. This is the sixth holy number.

Animalis (Latin): that which has breath. From *anima* (Latin): breath. Also spirit, soul.

Breath is the wind that moves you; what does it matter if it fills your lungs of flesh or bottles? I have lungs of flesh, I have a stomach. What is a soul made of?

Do you have a soul? Do I?

The breath gives me voice. The fish is mute, the comet breathless; I haven't heard any voice but my own in so long.

Are you there? Are you lonely?

When I was a little boy I saw a comet in the sky and thought: Wings are not enough to fly, but if you catch a comet with a bug net, well . . . Well, that might just do the trick.

Breath gives life. To live: the way I keep my face on, my voice in, my soul from spilling out.

Night already. Look, there is a light in the black above. It is a comet; see its long tail? Like a rose blooming in the sky.

If we catch it, maybe we can fly.

Tomorrow I think I'll walk into the sea, swim as far as I can.

And then what?

Then, nothing. I let go.

Instead of walking into the sea, in the morning Theo started building a new animal. He put up a tent just outside the fuselage, using some leftover tarpaulin and steel rods from the craft. He gathered all his materials inside: tubes, wire, bottles, cable ties, remains of beasts that had drowned in the past, or ones which had been created with some fundamental flaw that never allowed them to live in the first place. Theo worked quickly but carefully, pausing every now and then to steady his trembling hands, to blink the blurriness away. New sores appeared on his chest, but he ignored them.

This one would live. Perhaps it would even fly.

The rest of the beasts gathered outside the makeshift tent, as if to witness the birth of their kin.

g=36,7. This is the seventh holy number.

Come here, friend. Sit. Get some rest. I can see your knees trembling, your hip ready to give, your feet digging into the mud. Soon you will die, if you stay this way.

I see you have a spine, friend.

I, too, have a spine.

Theo was out fishing when the clouds started to gather and the sea turned black. Storms were not rare on Oceanus, but this one looked angrier than usual. He shouldered his fishing gear and started treading water towards the shore. He passed Animalis Elegans, its wings undulating faster and faster, and Animalis Caecus, which seemed to pause to look at him through its mechanical blindness, its nose pointed at the sky.

Theo made sure the half-finished beast was resting as securely as possible under the tarpaulin, and withdrew in the fuselage for what was to come.

h=65,7. This is the eighth holy number.

Once, a long long time ago, there was a prophet in old Earth who asked: when we have cut down all the trees and scraped the galaxy clean of stars, what will be left to shelter us from the terrible, empty skies?

Theo watched from his safe spot behind the fuselage's porthole as the beasts hammered their tails to the ground to defend their skeletons against the rising winds. Soon, everything outside was a blur of sand and rain. The craft was being battered from all sides; by the time the storm subsided, it would be half-buried in sand and kelp. And there was nothing to do but watch as the wind dislodged the rod that marked Tessa's grave and the red scarf was blown away, soon nowhere to be seen. It disappeared into the sea as if it had never existed at all, as if it had only been a memory of a childish story from long-ago and far-away. There was nothing to do as the wind uprooted the tarpaulin tent and blew the new animal to pieces; nothing to do as Animalis Elegans was torn from the ground and dragged to the water, its silken wings crushed under the waves.

Theo walked over to the trapdoor, cracked it open to let in some air. The night, heavy and humid, stuck to his skin.

i=49. This is the ninth holy number.

The night is heavy and humid like the dreams I used to have as a boy. In my dream, I see I'm walking into the sea, only it's not the sea any more, it's tall grass, taller than any grass I've ever seen in any ecosystem, taller than me, taller than the beasts. I swim in the grass, and it grows even taller; it reaches my head and keeps growing towards the sky, or maybe it's me getting smaller and smaller until all I can see is grass above and around me. I fall back, and the grass catches me, and it's the sky catching me like I always knew it would.

The storm lasted two Oceanus days and two Oceanus nights. When the clouds parted and the winds moved deeper into the ocean, Theo finally emerged from the fuselage. Half the beach had turned into a mire. Animalis Elegans was nowhere in sight. Animalis Primus limped in the distance. The beach was strewn with parts; only three of the beasts had survived the storm.

"No point in mourning, ja?" Theo muttered, and got to work.

He gathered as many of the materials as had landed in the area around the craft, dismantled the remains of the new animal that would never be named.

He had laid everything on the tarpaulin to dry, when a glimpse of white caught his eye. He turned towards the expanse of sea that blended into mire, and squinted. At first he thought it was foam, but no; it was one of Elegans's wings, a precious piece of white silk poking out of a murky-looking patch in the ground.

He knew better than to go retrieve it, but he went anyway.

j=50. This is the tenth holy number.

Listen, listen. It's okay. Don't fret. Take it in. The desolation, take it all in. Decomposition is a vital part of any ecosystem. It releases nutrients that can be reused, returns to the atmosphere what was only borrowed before. Without it, dead matter would accumulate and the world would be fragmented and dead, a wasteland of drowned parts and things with no knees, no spine, no wings.

Theo had his hands on the precious fabric, knee-deep in the muck, when he realized he was sinking, inch by inch, every time he moved. He tried to pull himself back out, but the next moment the sand was up to his thighs. He tried to kick his way out, to drag himself up, but his knees buckled, his muscles burned and he sank deeper and deeper with every breath he took.

This is it, then, he thought. *Here we are, friend. Here we are.*

He let out a breath, and it was almost like letting go.

k=61,9. This is the last holy number.

So here we are, friend: I, *Homo Necans,* the Man who Dies; you, ever a corpse. Beautiful, exquisite corpse. I lay my hands on you, caress your inanimate flawlessness. I dip my palms into you, what you once were. And then, there it is, so close and tangible I can almost reach it.

Here I am.

In your soul up to my knees.

The sand around Theo was drying in the sun. It was up to his navel now. Wouldn't be long. The wind hissed against the kelp and sand, lulling him. His eyes closed and he dozed off, still holding on to the wing.

He was woken by the rattling sound of Animalis Primus limping towards him.

The beast approached, its feet distributing its weight so as to barely touch the unsteady sand.

"I made you fine, didn't I?" Theo mused. "Just fine."

Primus came to a halt next to Theo, and waited.

He looked up at the beast, squinting at the sun behind it. "What are you doing, old friend?" he asked.

The beast stood, as if waiting for him to reach out, to hold on.

Theo pulled a hand out of the sand and reached for the beast's first knees. He was afraid he might trip the animal over, take them both down, but as soon as he got a firm grasp on its skeleton, Primus started walking against the wind, pulling Theo out of the sand.

He let go once he was safely away from the marsh. He collapsed on the powdery sand, trying to catch his breath, reel it back in, keep it from running out. Animalis Primus did not stop.

"Wait," Theo whispered as he pulled himself half-way up from the ground, thousands of minuscule grains sticking to his damp cheek. The beast marched onwards, unresponsive. "Wait!" Theo shouted, with all the breath he had left. He almost passed out.

The wind changed direction. Theo rested his head back on the sand, spent, and watched as Animalis Primus walked away—all clank and mechanics and the vestige of something like breath.

ABOUT THE AUTHOR

Natalia Theodoridou is currently a PhD Candidate at the School of Oriental and African Studies, University of London. Originally from Greece, she has lived and studied in the USA, UK, and Indonesia for several years.

Natalia was the Grand Prize winner for Prose of Spark Contest Three. Her short fiction and poetry have appeared or are forthcoming in such publications as *Strange Horizons, Ideomancer, Spark Anthology IV*, and *Eye to the Telescope,* among others. She is a first reader for *Goldfish Grimm's Spicy Fiction Sushi.*

And Wash Out by Tides of War

AN OWOMOYELA

I am sitting at the top of the spire of the Observance of the War, one of three memorials equidistant from the Colony Center. The soles of my runners' grips are pressed against the spire's composite, their traction engineered at a microscopic level. But I'm not going to push off. I'm 180 meters up, and while I could drop and catch the festoons—my gloves get as much traction as my grips—that's not what I want. I want to freefall all 180 meters, and catch myself, and launch into a run.

That's crazy thinking. I'm good, but no human's *that* good; I'm a freerunner, not a hhaellesh.

I shift my center of gravity. The wind is still temperate up here, fluttering cool under my collar. It outlines the spot of heat where my pendant rests against my skin.

The pendant is the size of my thumbnail, and always warmer than it should be. This has something to do with it reflecting the heat of my body back to me, so the pendant itself never heats up. It was built to do this because it's no gem; its brilliant red comes from my mother's cryopreserved blood.

It was, until the Feast of the Return that morning, the only thing I'd known of her.

The colony's designed for freerunning. The cops all take classes in it. That's what comes of a government that worships the hhaellesh, who can carve their own path through the three dimensions.

I'm not a cop, either.

I end up dropping, twisting so my fingers and toes find the carved laurels, and from there I make a second drop to the Observance's dome. At my hip, my phone starts thumping like an artificial heartbeat. I pause with my fingertips on the gilt, and finally turn to brace my heels against the shingles and lean back into the curve. I clip the hands-free to my ear, and thumb the respond button. Then I just listen.

After a moment of silence, a human voice says, *"Aditi?"*

I let out a breath. "Michel," I answer. He's a friend.

"Are you okay—?"

"I don't want to talk about it." Obviously a hhaellesh could get up to my perch here, and so could Michel—he's from a family of cops, so he's been playing games with gravity for longer than I have. But effective or not, there's a reason I'm nearly two hundred meters up, and that reason has a lot to do with not wanting to talk about how okay I am.

Michel digests that, then says *"Okay. Did you hear the new Elías Perez episode?"*

My chest fills with a relief indistinguishable from love. I love Michel so much that it's painful, sometimes, to know he's not my brother. I wish the same blood flowed through both our bodies, and without thinking past that, my fingers go to the pendant at my throat. There, my voice catches.

There are moments when I feel so ashamed.

"I haven't," I say. "Put it on."

The hhaellesh stand at least six feet tall, and usually closer to seven or eight. Their skin is glossy black. Their digitigrade feet end in small, grasping pads; their hands end in two fingers and two opposing thumbs which are thin enough to fit into cracks and gaps and strong enough to pierce titanium composite and tear apart the alloys of landships. They are streamlined and swift, with aquiline profiles and a leaping, running gait like a cat or an impala. They can fall from high atmosphere and suffer no injury. They can jump sixteen meters in a bound. They are war machines and killing machines.

They are also human sacrifices.

I envy them.

Gods, if there was anything in the universe Elías couldn't handle, his writers haven't thrown it at him yet. He would know how to tell his best friend about an enlistment option. He could figure out how to deal with a hhaellesh showing up at his door.

Michel starts the playback, and I tweak the audio balance so I can hear Michel breathing while we both listen. The serials are propaganda and we know it, but they're enjoyable propaganda, so that's fine.

[The esshesh gave us the hhaellesh and the hhaellesh handed us the war—but if we didn't have the hhaellesh, we'd still have Elías Perez,] the

canned narrator says, and I lean into the backbeat behind his words. *[Welcome to the adventure.]*

Around me, the colony spreads out in its careful geometry. There's nothing left to chance or whimsy, here, or adapted from the streets and carriageways built by another, more ancient, society. There's no downtown you can look at and say, *this predated cars and light rail.* No sprawling tourist docks with names that hold onto history. This place is older than I am, but not by much; it's only about the age of my mother.

That's why we cling so much to ceremony, I think: it's what we have in place of tradition. We make monuments to an ongoing war, and when the soldiers return home we have feasts, and we plan holidays to rename the Observances to the Remembrances. The war's only just ended and in a month we'll have three Remembrances of the War, in shiny white limestone and black edging in places of honor.

I get it.

Seriously, I do. When you don't have history in the place you live, you have to make it up or go insane.

Earlier in the day, my mother'd shown up to the crappy little allotment I cook and sleep in but don't spend much time in. My allotment's on the seventeenth floor of a housing unit, which makes for a perfect launch point, and doesn't usually get me visitors on the balcony. I was on the mat in my room, with my mattress folded up into the wall, doing pushup jump squats. They weren't helping. I'd split my lip just a bit earlier, and since I bite when I get restless, I had the taste of blood in my mouth.

Then there she was, knocking at the lintel, and I split my lip open again.

I did a thirty-second cooldown and made myself walk to the window. If it had been dark, if the light hadn't been scattering off the white buildings and back down from the cyan sky, it might not have glinted on her skin. She might have just been a black, alien shape like a hole in the world.

"I expected to see you at the Feast of the Return," she said. "I registered my arrival."

"I was busy," I lied.

She regarded me, quietly. And although I didn't want to, I invited her in.

When I first met Michel, he was walking along the rails of the pedestrian bridge by the Second General Form school. I was in Second General Form mostly because my father had hired a tutor before we came to the colony; my education in Shivaji Administrative District hadn't exactly

24

been compatible with the colony's educational tracks. I was new, and didn't know any of my classmates. We knew each other's names from the class introductions, so Michel didn't bother to introduce himself.

"Settle an argument," he said. "I think Elías is in love with Seve, and Seve just thinks he's ridiculous. My cousin thinks Seve loves Elías but doesn't want to show it, and Elías is just friendly and chirpy to everyone, so he doesn't even see anything weird about acting like that at Seve. You should tell her I'm right."

I shook my head. "Elías? Is that the government stuff? I don't listen to that."

"Wha-a-at?" Michel asked, bobbing the *a*. "Come on, *everyone* listens to Elías!"

"My dad says it's just propaganda," I said, and I remember that little preadolescent me felt damn proud of herself and all smart and grown-up to be slinging around words like *propaganda*. "They just make it so people will want to join the war."

"Well, duh," Michel said. "Everybody *knows* that. But it's cool! Come on, lemme tell you about this time that Elías got stuck on this planet; they were trying to make it into a colony, but there was a whole swarm of the enemy and his ship was broken and he couldn't take off . . . "

Elías always found a way through, and by the end of the day, I was listening to the show. I never helped Michel settle his argument, but I came to my own conclusions.

Today's episode opens with the soundscape that means Elías is on the bridge of the Command and Control station in the sector designated as the Front. Meaning he's on the front lines. Last time that happened, he was in a story arc that had him working with the Coalition forces, which he hates to do; Elías isn't really an official sort of guy.

[*"If our intelligence reports are correct,"*] says the voice of Commodore Shah, [*"we're about to lose the war."*]

The art of the gentle lead-in is verboten in Elías Perez.

[*"A larger enemy presence than any we've ever seen is massing at Huracán II. We believe they'll use this staging ground to launch a major, unified offensive on the colonies."*]

[*"You want us to what?"*] That's Seve, the captain of Elías's ship. She snickers. [*"Take out a whole fleet of the bastids? Hah. No bones in that dog."*]

"Oh, Seve," Michel says. Seve's got a stack of sayings that only make sense to her—and to Elías, nowadays, though they didn't always. Elías and Seve have been partners since episode 3, where Elías stowed aboard Seve's pirate ship and ended up saving it when it was infested by the enemy. Seve turned around and said, there, that paid Elías's boarding fee; what was he going to pay for passage?

I'm a fan of Elías and Seve. Love at first uncompromising deal. And she isn't the kind to think the end of the war obligates her into anything.

[*"If their war force goes unopposed, the enemy will be able to sweep through our territories unopposed. The Coalition doesn't have the fleet strength to stop them."*]

There's a subtle swell in the background music, a rumble of drums and solar radio output, and a thrill goes through me. The writers can play drama with our fear of the war: for most of us, it's the fun kind of fear where something is technically possible but pretty damn unlikely, like an asteroid crashing into the colony. After we lost the Painter settlement, the war was always off somewhere *out there*; we sent out troops, we made our hhaellesh, but it's not like we were really under threat of invasion. I don't think our colony even had an invasion plan in place, beyond the esshesh defense emplacements. We all got a little afraid, but the fear was a *what if, on an offchance, someday . . .* and not a *when, as it will, this happens to us.*

[*"Okay,"*] Elías says, always the good guy, always the hero. [*"What's our job? We can barely take one enemy ship in a firefight; a force that size is beyond us."*]

Commodore Shah says nothing, and the delay is striking. The audio play doesn't go for delays. There's another rumble, and another sensation thrills up my spine, but it's not the fun kind of thrill this time.

"Oh, you're not," I whisper.

[*"As you know,"*] Shah says, her voice clipped so regret doesn't make it through. [*"Huracán II suffers from a violent geology. Your ship is one of the few with both the range to reach the Huracán system and the maneuverability to penetrate the enemy's lines and engage your jump engines within the planet's red jump threshold."*]

I hear Michel's sucked-in breath, and I'm sitting dumb, myself.

[*"Blow out the planet and us with it,"*] Seve says. [*"Jump'll turn the rock into a frag grenade, and the gravity turns my girl's engines into a nova. That what you want from us, Shah?"*]

Shah's always looked after her people. Elías and Seve—they're not official, military types, but Shah looks after them as her own. Problem is, even Shah's people come in second to the war.

[*"It's not what I want,"*] Shah says, and I want to slam my headset down. [*"But I don't see another option."*]

"They're doing a finale," I say, my calves and fingers burning again to run. "The war is over, so they're just going to finish Elías Perez."

"You left when I was three years old," I'd told my mother as she crouched at the edge of the table, as I shuffled through my shelves for a decent tea. I had a couple spoonfuls left of loose-leaf colony Faisal, which I hear is a good substitute for an Earth Assam, which I will never in my life be able to afford unless it goes big and all the importers start shipping it in in bulk. But the urge to make a good impression got in a fistfight with the urge to be petty and spiteful, and I pulled out two bags of a generic colony black and plunked them into mugs.

"I remember," she said. "I braided your hair and you wore your favorite dress. It was the blue of cobalt glass."

Her voice was deep and flanged, and totally factual. All hhaellesh sound alike. At least, the ones on the war reports sounded the same as my mother.

I have an allotment and not a flat because I have a work placement and not a career. I don't care for any of the careers on offer. But the colony's not so much of a fool to let work potential go unexploited, unlike the governments of Earth which I'm just old enough to remember. I still have images of walking to the subway past the grimy homeless, with my father's hand on the small of my back to rush me along.

That's what I remember of my childhood. My father's protective hand, my father's tutoring after school, my father's anchor mustache with a bit more salt in its pepper every year, my father's voice carefully explaining the war.

"I don't like dresses," I told my mother, and set down the two mugs of tea. Her fingers clicked around the ceramic.

The hhaellesh can eat and drink, but human scientists still don't know how food passes through the suits. We do know that the suits filter and metabolize any toxins—people have tried to poison them before, with everything from arsenic and cyanide to things like strong sulphuric acid, and the hhaellesh just eat and drink it up and are polite enough not to mention it.

I did not try to poison my mother.

"You've grown," she said. "Of course, I expected that."

"Yeah, kids grow up when you disappear on them."

She was quiet for a few seconds. "I did not expect your father to die."

I stared down into my slowly-darkening tea.

"I received notice," she said. "I had to make the decision whether or not to come home. The tide of the war hadn't turned yet. I knew the colony would look after you."

I swirled the tea in my mug. Tendrils of relative darkness wavered out from the bag.

"I was one of only eight hundred hhaellesh volunteers at that point," she said.

"Yeah, I know," I finally interrupted. "Without the hhaellesh, we wouldn't've won the war."

This is how the hhaellesh happened:

We had a handful of colonies in the Solar system and three outside of it: Gliese, Korolev, and Painter. Then, abruptly, we had a handful of colonies in the Solar system and two colonies in Gliese and Korolev.

We still thought interstellar colonization was a pretty neat thing, and despite centuries of space war fiction, we didn't have the infrastructure or the technology to mount a space war. We were thoroughly thumped.

Then the esshesh showed up and told us that, while war was (untranslatable, but we think against their religion), they had no problems with arming races to defend themselves.

So they gave us the hhaellesh.

This is how the hhaellesh work:

There's a black suit that scatters light like obsidian and feels like a flexible atmosphere-dome composite to the touch. A soldier gets inside, bare as the day she was born. The suit closes around her.

In a few minutes, it's taking her breath and synthesizing the carbon dioxide back to oxygen. In a few hours it's taking her waste and digesting the organic components. In a few days it's replaced the top layers of her skin. In a few months it's integrated itself into her muscles. In a few years there's nothing human left in there, just the patterns of her neural activity playing across an alien substrate that we haven't managed to understand yet.

This is how a hhaellesh retires:

The suit has a reverse mode. It can start rebuilding the human core, re-growing the body, replacing the armor's substrate material with blood and muscle and bone and brain matter until the armor opens up again, and the human steps out, bare as the day they were born. A body like Theseus's ship.

But to do that, it needs the original human DNA.

Or some human DNA, in any case; hell, I don't know that anyone's tried it, but you could probably feed in the DNA of your favorite celebrity and the hhaellesh suit would grow it for you, slipping your brain pattern in like that was nothing strange. I suppose that should freak me out—y'know, existentially—more than just growing a new copy of a body long ago digested by an alien non-meatsuit.

It probably should, but it doesn't.

This is how a hhaellesh tries to *get* the DNA that'll let it retire:

My mother crouched at the side of my table. With the inhuman height and the swept-back digitigrade legs, the chairs weren't designed to accommodate her.

"When I left, I entrusted you with a sample of my DNA," she said, and my hand went to the pendant. "With love, my daughter, I ask for it back."

At that point, I dove out the window.

"They *can't* cancel Elías," I say. The top-of-spire restlessness is back, and I want to drop, freefall, roll, clamber, climb. My shoulders and thighs are shaking. "The fuck. He's a goddamn cultural phenomenon, by now."

Michel's voice is unsteady as well, but not as much as mine. He doesn't get it. *"To be fair, I feel like after you've won the war you don't need to push people to sign up for the Forces any more."*

"Fuck the war," I say, and there's anger at the pit of my throat. Like: how dare they take this away from us. Like: Elías and his adventures belong to us. Since the beginning of the war they've been how we're meant to see ourselves—clever and active and *go team human*. You can't take away our stories just because we won.

The first time I met my mother—

Except I can't put it like that, can I? You don't really meet your mother. Or I guess maybe you do at the moment of conception, if you think your zygote is you, or maybe it's when the first glimmers of thought show up in your still-developing brain. But I think maybe it doesn't count if there's no chance that little undeveloped you won't retain the memory.

So. The first time I met my mother, I was in a utility transitway. You know, what we have for back alleys.

I've always been the kid with a chip on her shoulder and a grudge against the world and her nose high in the air. The grudge and the pride come from the same thing. Neither made me many friends.

I ran into a bunch of the voluntary-career types in the transitway on the morning of the Feast, just after the big public ceremony. My blood was up and they were them, and, well, the specifics of the argument don't really matter. I started it. And then I was in the comforting beat of a street fight, and with a split lip and three split knuckles, and while one of them was hollering about how he was going to file a complaint for misdemeanor assault, who should show up?

And my heart leapt up and got a grip in my throat, and I thought, *Oh gods, a hhaellesh,* and standing right there, alien and beautiful. Staring at us with a blank, featureless swept-forward face that we all unambiguously read as disapproval.

The fight stopped. The boys stood there, twitching and uneasy, until they worked out that the hhaellesh was only staring at me. Then they slipped away.

And I stood there, frozen in the moment, until *I* worked out why a hhaellesh would single me out and come find me in a utility transitway. The wonder was slapped right out of me. It meant nothing: it wasn't the free choice of an alien intelligence but the obligate bonds of unreliable blood.

I turned my back and sprinted away.

. . . hold it there for a moment. I realize this makes it sound like I just run from all my problems, and I want to make it clear that that's not true. The truth is that I run from this *one* problem, and looking back at it, I guess I always have.

I was talking about my pride and my grudge, and how they both come down to this pendant at the base of my throat. My mother's blood. My mother the hhaellesh, the guardian of the colonies, the war hero.

All the hhaellesh are war heroes.

What the hell am I?

[*"My gotdamn ship,"*] Seve says. They're in the corridors of *her gotdamn ship* now, the soundscape full of mechanical noises and ambiance. There was a behind-the-scenes episode a few months ago back where they talked about those soundscapes, and how they chose the sounds for Seve's ship to be reminiscent of a heartbeat, rushing blood, ventilation like breath, so it'd seem alive. [*"My gotdamn job. Better pilot than you, anyway; I can see this idiot plan through."*] She's pissed-off. I would be. Hell, I am.

[*"I'm a good enough pilot to dodge through a crowd,"*] Elías says. [*"Come on, Seve. The captain doesn't have to go down with her ship."*]

Michel complains a lot that Seve is a boy's name, and I tell him that so were Sasha and Madison and Wyatt, back in the pre-space days known as the depths of history. And then Michel says that of course I would pay attention to the pre-space days, and I say that of course he thinks history started with the erection of the initial colony dome.

Michel is first-generation colony native. He was born here. His parents were in the third or fourth batch of colonists to set down here. We're never quite sure who's supposed to be jealous of who in this relationship, so mostly we just rib each other a lot.

In my position, it's easy to feel like you don't have a history. Yeah, I'm from Earth, but I don't remember much. My dad knew more, but he naturalized us; the most culture I think he held over was the way he made tea in a pot with colony spices, and his habit of saying *gods* instead of *god*.

I'm the girl with the hhaellesh mother and the blood at her throat. That's who I am. And I was pretty sure no one could take that away.

["Seve, I can't let you die in my place,"] Elías says.

Seven snorts. *["Well, one of us got to."]*

"I enlisted," I blurt out. I swing the words like a fist. And I can hear the change in Michel's breathing on the other end; I can hear how Elías and the finale and how the writers are screwing us over has ceased to matter.

"Say what?"

"I enlisted," I say again. "I got the assessment. They were going to let me into a Basic Training Group and then the war ended."

Michel doesn't know what to say. I can tell because he says *"You—"*, and then *"Oh."*, and then *"So . . . what? What now? Are you—"* and then he trails off into silence. I'm pretty sure I've hurt him.

It's a thing, in my family.

"I don't know," I say. All my plans have been derailed. "I can join the colony's military track. Would that be totally pointless? Think I should go? I could just get out of here."

". . . should I know the answer to this?" He gives a nervous laugh—and the laugh is probably fake, now that I think about it. It's not right, anyway. Michel's real laugh is this deep, throaty thing that doesn't sound right when you know that his voice is higher than average and naturally polite.

If Michel was blood family there'd be a reason I could point to as why I felt so close to him, without wanting to screw him. I could have family that meant what family's supposed to mean.

After a moment, he says *"Aditi, if this is about your mother, can we just, maybe, talk about your mother?"*

Michel, Michel, my not-family family. Talking about my mother, my family not-family. I got this far by not looking too close at the contradiction. It's a lot harder to do when it breaks up your fights and shows up to tea.

It's a lot harder to do when it wins *its* fucking war.

• • •

When we came to the Colony, my father and I, we stepped off the transport in a queue of seven hundred other colonists. We waited nearly an hour before it was our turn to go into a white room whose windows let in the blue of the sky and the white of the skyline, and a pleasant-enough woman took our biometric data and verified all my father's professional assessments. She gave him his schedules —for Colony orientation, the walking tour, the commerce and services lecture, the first day at his assigned career—and set up an educational track for me. Through all of it, I was bored but fascinated by the blue-white-green of the outside world, and my father bounced me on his knee.

At the end, the woman bent down and put her face in front of mine. "That's a beautiful piece of jewelry," she said. "What is it?"

I looked her straight in the eye, and said—you know, in the way that some kids don't quite get metaphor, even when they're using it —"It's my mother."

On my phone, there's a message from the Coalition Armed Forces Enlistment Office. It reads:

> *To Aditi Elizabeth Chattopadhyay,*
> This is a note to confirm that your assessment scores were sufficient to place you in a Basic Training Group for Immediate Interstellar and Exo-Atmospheric Combat. However, due to the recent decision of the Colony Coalition Oversight Office and the cessation of hostilities, the Coalition Armed Forces as an oversight unit is being disbanded and the colonies' individual standing military forces are being scaled back.
>
> *At your request, your application can be transferred to the Gliese Armed Forces Enlistment Office, where you can enter into their Standing Military career track. If no such request is made, we will consider your enlistment withdrawn.*
>
> *Thank you for your willingness to serve the safety and security of the Colonies.*

The Standing Military career track trains you in an off-surface location with strict access restrictions. I could still get out of here. I have the option. She can't take everything away.

I dial back the Elías audio to a quiet background murmur. I can't concentrate on it, anyway, and I don't want to. I don't want to hear Elías and Seve argue about who'll sacrifice for the other.

"*Aditi,*" Michel says.

"Why the *hell*," I ask him, "wouldn't you just put your blood in a bank safe if it meant that godsdamn much to you?"

There's a moment when I think that could have used a little more context than I gave it, but Michel finds the meaning fast. "*If I had a kid, I'd want to leave something they could know me by.*"

I kinda think there's not a maternal bone in my body, because that just sounds stupid to me. "Yeah, well, I didn't end up knowing her, did I?"

"*You can, though. Now. Can't you?*"

"She came back for her *blood*," I say. "She never said she came back to get to know me."

Like a slap in the face, Michel laughs.

"What the fuck," I tell him. "Not funny."

"*It is, though,*" Michel says. "*Adi, I swear you just described exactly what you would do. You would go off to war and kick ass and come back home when there was no more ass to kick, and be all 'hi, I'm back, gimme.' Tell me you wouldn't.*"

I spluttered.

[*"Some things are more important than my life, Seve!"*], Elías is shouting, though the low volume just makes him sound faraway and muffled like he's already lost.

From the beginning, Seve has said that if she can't save herself, she's not worth saving. And this is propaganda, so the story never goes out of its way to correct her. I like that. I like that she's never needed saving when she couldn't save herself.

I don't like change.

I want to mute the audio.

"I'm not that self-centered," I tell Michel, but my hand is on my pendant and I've convinced myself the blood inside is mine. It's demonstrably *not* mine, and the DNA will prove it. But still. Still.

"*Adi, can I tell you something, and not get in a fistfight with you in a utility transitway?*"

I've never been in a fight with Michel. "What?"

He takes a moment to put the words together. "*The necklace is just a thing, Adi. Get your mom back. Once you have her, you can replace the blood. Anyway, one necklace for one mom is a pretty good trade.*"

Theseus's pendant. I feel a rush of disagreement. I guess that solves that philosophical riddle for me: I really believe that if you replace all the boards, it's not the same ship.

Which means I also believe there's no way to keep the ship from eventually rotting away.

I never helped Michel settle his argument, but that doesn't mean I didn't come to my own conclusions.

I think Elías and Seve love each other, but love doesn't tell you what to do with it. It just shows up like a guest you have to make a bed for, and it puts everything out of order, and it makes demands.

I don't hear the rest of the episode.

I take my time. I breathe through the anger in my gut and the sense, not exhilarating now, of falling. Then, in the evening, I sync up with the colony directions database and do a search for hhaellesh in public areas.

Five hhaellesh arrived during the Feast of the Return, and two of them aren't hanging out anywhere that the public cams can see them. One of the ones who is is surrounded by children and a lady who looks like their mother, beaming the whole group of them. Of the other two, one is walking the gardens in the Colony Center Plaza, and the other is . . . familiar.

I take the monkey's route, as my father called it. Roof to roof and wall by wall, the colony's engineered and modified design giving me wings. From the feeds I read, the freerunning spirit everywhere means working with your environment, not against it; you have to take your obstacles as opportunities or you'll never get anywhere. Literally, at that.

If there's a lesson to be learned there and applied to the rest of my life, I've yet to learn it.

I pass over alleys and shopways and along the taut wires that traverse the wide boulevards, the places where parades had been held. People see me, but to them, I'm just motion; just another citizen who takes a hobbyist's interest in how to get around. Anonymous. Not Aditi, the girl with the hhaellesh mother, the girl with her mother's blood. They see me as I'm starting to see myself.

I run harder.

After my father's first day of work, he took me to the breadfruit shop. It's not real breadfruit—it's some native plant the first colony engineers analyzed and deemed edible; something that looked like a breadfruit to whichever one of them named it—but when it's processed and mashed it has a texture like firm ice cream and a taste that takes flavorings well. My father and I got bowls full of big, colorful scoops, and asked one of the other patrons to take a picture of us. They did, and said "Welcome to the colony!" We were that obvious.

We sent the picture to my mother, and that's where I find her today. Sitting at the table we always tried to get, without any of the breadfruit in front of her. Hhaellesh can eat, but I'm not sure they need to, and I have no idea if they have a sense of taste. You only hear about them eating to accept hospitality.

There's a halo of awed silence around her, and I slink through it and take another one of the chairs.

"I'm sorry," she says, and I let out a breath. Truth was, until she'd said that, I'd had some doubt that it was her. The hhaellesh all look alike.

I grumble something. I don't know how to accept her apology.

"I haven't been a good mother," my war hero says. "I don't know if you want me to start trying now. You've done well without me."

Yeah, if you want to call it that. I serve the minimum work requirements and spend the rest of my time running across the roofs and up the walls. I haven't gone out and won any wars in my free time.

What I've done, what they'll know me for if I touch the history books at all, is that I've carried *her*.

My fingers itch at the tips. I want to touch the pendant, but I don't. "Hhaellesh don't have blood, do they?"

"The armor substrate carries energy and nutrients," my mother says. "We don't need blood, unless . . . "

"Why do you want to be human?" I ask. *I* don't want to be human. I want to be more than what I am.

My mother doesn't answer that, and the stillness of the armor is the stillness of an alien thing: how am I to read it? Then she seems to answer two questions, my own and one she hasn't articulated.

Why don't you?

"I think," she says, and her words are careful, perhaps uncertain. "if you are something, you don't want it. Does that make sense? Because you *are* it, you forget ever wanting it. Or, I suppose, it never comes up."

I shake my head.

"I miss being human," she says. "I miss feeling warm and sleeping in and stretching out sore muscles. I miss holding you. You were so small, when I left." I think she watches me. "You regret not being old enough."

"*Old* enough?" I snap. For what? To remember her leaving?

My mother holds up her hand. "This lit me up like a candle," she said, turning those long, precise fingers. "I was a goddess. A fury, a valkyrie. I wanted this. Now I miss being human."

I grind my fingertips out against the table. "What's going to happen to the suit, if you're not using it?"

35

My mother lays her hand near mine, which is a disturbingly human gesture coming from something whose hand is a mechanical claw. "It'll go into a museum," she says. "Or on display in one of the Remembrances. I would give it to you if I could."

I rear back, at that.

"Ah," she says, and she can't smile. There's nothing on her face to smile. But I get the impression she's smiling. "You think I'd say, no, it wasn't worth it, in the end. I've learned my lesson and a human life is the most important thing of all. No." Her head bends toward the table. "This is a part of my life; this is me. I will not disavow it. I would give it to you if I could."

The colony is white buildings and boulevards, green growing plants, and the searing blue sky. And then there's the black of the esshesh artillery emplacements, the black edging on the Observances. Red's not a colony color. Red is primal and messy, like blood.

When I went to enlist, they took a hard-copy signature in black ink and a handprint biometric signature as well. I wonder what else the biometrics recorded: my anxiety? My anger? The thrumming of my heart in my veins?

My mother's hands are cool and pulseless on the table. Black as the artillery. Black as the ink. Black as the space between what stars we see, where the primal brightness of the cosmos has been stretched into infrared by the passage of time.

I reach behind my neck and fumble with the clasp of my pendant. It takes me a bit to work it out; it's stayed against my throat through showers and formal occasions and a hospital stay or two, busted ribs and broken legs. Pulling it off makes me feel more naked than taking my clothes off does. But here I am, baring myself in front of this alien who wants more intimacy than I think she deserves.

"Two conditions," I say. And it's difficult to tell, under the smooth black mask, but I think she's still watching *me* and not the blood. I push on ahead. "One: I want a piece of that armor. Or, I guess, the substrate. Make a pendant out of it."

It's not a replacement for the blood. But it's not something I'll be holding in trust: it's part of my history, now, too, and it's something that'll be *mine*.

My mother nods.

I exhale. Red's no good for the colony anyway. Black's a bit better, if only because black is the color of the hhaellesh, and the security emplacements which grow fractally more close-packed toward the colony's borders: the lines we draw around ourselves to protect us from the enemy.

After Painter, the enemy never set foot on colony land. They're not the thing that scares me. I'm still figuring out what my enemy is.

"Two," I say. And I'm not sure how to say this next part.

But those were her words. *I'd give it to you if I could.*

"I want your stories," I tell her.

ABOUT THE AUTHOR

An (pronounce it "On") **Owomoyela** is a neutrois author with a background in web development, linguistics, and weaving chain maille out of stainless steel fencing wire, whose fiction has appeared in a number of venues including *Clarkesworld, Asimov's, Lightspeed,* and a handful of Year's Bests. An's interests range from pulsars and Cepheid variables to gender studies and nonstandard pronouns, with a plethora of stops in-between. Se can be found online at an.owomoyela.net, and can be funded at patreon.com/an_owomoyela.

Infinities

VANDANA SINGH

An equation means nothing to me unless it expresses a thought of God.

—Srinivasa Ramanujan, Indian mathematician (1887-1920)

Abdul Karim is his name. He is a small, thin man, precise to the point of affectation in his appearance and manner. He walks very straight; there is gray in his hair and in his short, pointed beard. When he goes out of the house to buy vegetables, people on the street greet him respectfully. "Salaam, Master sahib," they say, or "Namaste, Master Sahib," according to the religion of the speaker. They know him as the mathematics master at the municipal school. He has been there so long that he sees the faces of his former students everywhere: the autorickshaw driver Ramdas who refuses to charge him, the man who sells paan from a shack at the street corner, with whom he has an account, who never reminds him when his payment is late—his name is Imran and he goes to the mosque far more regularly than Abdul Karim.

They all know him, the kindly mathematics master, but he has his secrets. They know he lives in the old yellow house, where the plaster is flaking off in chunks to reveal the underlying brick. The windows of the house are hung with faded curtains that flutter tremulously in the breeze, giving passersby an occasional glimpse of his genteel poverty—the threadbare covers on the sofa, the wooden furniture as gaunt and lean and resigned as the rest of the house, waiting to fall into dust. The house is built in the old-fashioned way about a courtyard, which is paved with brick except for a circular omission where a great litchi tree grows. There is a high wall around the courtyard, and one door in it that leads to the patch of wilderness that was once a vegetable garden. But the hands that tended it—his mother's hands—are no longer able to do more than hold

38

a mouthful of rice between the tips of the fingers, tremblingly conveyed to the mouth. The mother sits nodding in the sun in the courtyard while the son goes about the house, dusting and cleaning as fastidiously as a woman. The master has two sons—one is in distant America, married to a gori bibi, a white woman—how unimaginable! He never comes home and writes only a few times a year. The wife writes cheery letters in English that the master reads carefully with finger under each word. She talks about his grandsons, about baseball (a form of cricket, apparently), about their plans to visit, which never materialize. Her letters are as incomprehensible to him as the thought that there might be aliens on Mars, but he senses a kindness, a reaching out, among the foreign words. His mother has refused to have anything to do with that woman.

The other son has gone into business in Mumbai. He comes home rarely, but when he does he brings with him expensive things—a television set, an air-conditioner. The TV is draped reverently with an embroidered white cloth and dusted every day but the master can't bring himself to turn it on. There is too much trouble in the world. The air-conditioner gives him asthma so he never turns it on, even in the searing heat of summer. His son is a mystery to him—his mother dotes on the boy but the master can't help fearing that this young man has become a stranger, that he is involved in some shady business. The son always has a cell phone with him and is always calling nameless friends in Mumbai, bursting into cheery laughter, dropping his voice to a whisper, walking up and down the pathetically clean drawing-room as he speaks. Although he would never admit it to anybody other than Allah, Abdul Karim has the distinct impression that his son is waiting for him to die. He is always relieved when his son leaves.

Still, these are domestic worries. What father does not worry about his children? Nobody would be particularly surprised to know that the quiet, kindly master of mathematics shares them also. What they don't know is that he has a secret, an obsession, a passion that makes him different from them all. It is because of this, perhaps, that he seems always to be looking at something just beyond their field of vision, that he seems a little lost in the cruel, mundane world in which they live.

He wants to see infinity.

It is not strange for a mathematics master to be obsessed with numbers. But for Abdul Karim, numbers are the stepping stones, rungs in the ladder that will take him (Inshallah!) from the prosaic ugliness of the world to infinity.

When he was a child he used to see things from the corners of his eyes. Shapes moving at the very edge of his field of vision. Haven't we all felt that there was someone to our left or right, darting away when we turned our heads? In his childhood he had thought they were farishte, angelic beings keeping a watch over him. And he had felt secure, loved, nurtured by a great, benign, invisible presence.

One day he asked his mother:

"Why don't the farishte stay and talk to me? Why do they run away when I turn my head?"

Inexplicably to the child he had been, this innocent question led to visits to the Hakim. Abdul Karim had always been frightened of the Hakim's shop, the walls of which were lined from top to bottom with old clocks. The clocks ticked and hummed and whirred while tea came in chipped glasses and there were questions about spirits and possessions, and bitter herbs were dispensed in antique bottles that looked at though they contained djinns. An amulet was given to the boy to wear around his neck; there were verses from the Qur'an he was to recite every day. The boy he had been sat at the edge of the worn velvet seat and trembled; after two weeks of treatment, when his mother asked him about the farishte, he had said:

"They're gone."

That was a lie.

My theory stands as firm as a rock; every arrow directed against it will quickly return to the archer. How do I know this? Because I have studied it from all sides for many years; because I have examined all objections which have ever been made against the infinite numbers; and above all because I have followed its roots, so to speak, to the first infallible cause of all created things.

—Georg Cantor, German mathematician (1845-1918)

In a finite world, Abdul Karim ponders infinity. He has met infinities of various kinds in mathematics. If mathematics is the language of Nature, then it follows that there are infinities in the physical world around us as well. They confound us because we are such limited things. Our lives, our science, our religions are all smaller than the cosmos. Is the cosmos infinite? Perhaps. As far as we are concerned, it might as well be.

In mathematics there is the sequence of natural numbers, walking like small, determined soldiers into infinity. But there are less obvious infinities as well, as Abdul Karim knows. Draw a straight line, mark zero on one end and the number one at the other. How many numbers between zero and one? If you start counting now, you'll still be counting

40

when the universe ends, and you'll be nowhere near one. In your journey from one end to the other you'll encounter the rational numbers and the irrational numbers, most notably the transcendentals. The transcendental numbers are the most intriguing—you can't generate them from integers by division, or by solving simple equations. Yet in the simple number line there are nearly impenetrable thickets of them; they are the densest, most numerous of all numbers. It is only when you take certain ratios like the circumference of a circle to its diameter, or add an infinite number of terms in a series, or negotiate the countless steps of infinite continued fractions, do these transcendental numbers emerge. The most famous of these is, of course, pi, 3.14159 . . . , where there is an infinity of non-repeating numbers after the decimal point. The transcendentals! Theirs is a universe richer in infinities than we can imagine.

In finiteness—in that little stick of a number line—there is infinity. What a deep and beautiful concept, thinks Abdul Karim! Perhaps there are infinities in us too, universes of them.

The prime numbers are another category that capture his imagination. The atoms of integer arithmetic, the select few that generate all other integers, as the letters of an alphabet generate all words. There are an infinite number of primes, as befits what he thinks of as God's alphabet . . .

How ineffably mysterious the primes are! They seem to occur at random in the sequence of numbers: 2, 3, 5, 7, 11 . . . There is no way to predict the next number in the sequence without actually testing it. No formula that generates all the primes. And yet, there is a mysterious regularity in these numbers that has eluded the greatest mathematicians of the world. Glimpsed by Riemann, but as yet unproven, there are hints of order so deep, so profound, that it is as yet beyond us.

To look for infinity in an apparently finite world—what nobler occupation for a human being, and one like Abdul Karim, in particular?

As a child he questioned the elders at the mosque: What does it mean to say that Allah is simultaneously one, and infinite? When he was older he read the philosophies of Al Kindi and Al Ghazali, Ibn Sina and Iqbal, but his restless mind found no answers. For much of his life he has been convinced that mathematics, not the quarrels of philosophers, is the key to the deepest mysteries.

He wonders whether the farishte that have kept him company all his life know the answer to what he seeks. Sometimes, when he sees one at the edge of his vision, he asks a question into the silence. Without turning around.

Is the Riemann Hypothesis true?

Silence.

Are prime numbers the key to understanding infinity?

Silence.

Is there a connection between transcendental numbers and the primes?

There has never been an answer.

But sometimes, a hint, a whisper of a voice that speaks in his mind. Abdul Karim does not know whether his mind is playing tricks upon him or not, because he cannot make out what the voice is saying. He sighs and buries himself in his studies.

He reads about prime numbers in Nature. He learns that the distribution of energy level spacings of excited uranium nuclei seem to match the distribution of spacings between prime numbers. Feverishly he turns the pages of the article, studies the graphs, tries to understand. How strange that Allah has left a hint in the depths of atomic nuclei! He is barely familiar with modern physics—he raids the library to learn about the structure of atoms.

His imagination ranges far. Meditating on his readings, he grows suspicious now that perhaps matter is infinitely divisible. He is beset by the notion that maybe there is no such thing as an elementary particle. Take a quark and it's full of preons. Perhaps preons themselves are full of smaller and smaller things. There is no limit to this increasingly fine graininess of matter.

How much more palatable this is than the thought that the process stops somewhere, that at some point there is a pre-preon, for example, that is composed of nothing else but itself. How fractally sound, how beautiful if matter is a matter of infinitely nested boxes.

There is a symmetry in it that pleases him. After all, there is infinity in the very large too. Our universe, ever expanding, apparently without limit.

He turns to the work of Georg Cantor, who had the audacity to formalize the mathematical study of infinity. Abdul Karim painstakingly goes over the mathematics, drawing his finger under every line, every equation in the yellowing textbook, scribbling frantically with his pencil. Cantor is the one who discovered that certain infinite sets are more infinite than others—that there are tiers and strata of infinity. Look at the integers, 1, 2, 3, 4 . . . Infinite, but of a lower order of infinity than the real numbers like 1.67, 2.93 etc. Let us say the set of integers is of order Aleph-null, the set of real numbers of order Aleph-One, like the hierarchical ranks of a king's courtiers. The question that plagued

Cantor and eventually cost him his life and sanity was the Continuum Hypothesis, which states that there is no infinite set of numbers with order *between* Aleph-Null and Aleph-One. In other words, Aleph-One succeeds Aleph-Null; there is no intermediate rank. But Cantor could not prove this.

He developed the mathematics of infinite sets. Infinity plus infinity equals infinity. Infinity minus infinity equals infinity. But the Continuum Hypothesis remained beyond his reach.

Abdul Karim thinks of Cantor as a cartographer in a bizarre new world. Here the cliffs of infinity reach endlessly toward the sky, and Cantor is a tiny figure lost in the grandeur, a fly on a precipice. And yet, what boldness! What spirit! To have the gall to actually *classify* infinity . . .

His explorations take him to an article on the mathematicians of ancient India. They had specific words for large numbers. One purvi, a unit of time, is seven hundred and fifty-six thousand billion years. One sirsaprahelika is eight point four million Purvis raised to the twenty-eighth power. What did they see that caused them to play with such large numbers? What vistas were revealed before them? What wonderful arrogance possessed them that they, puny things, could dream so large?

He mentions this once to his friend, a Hindu called Gangadhar, who lives not far away. Gangadhar's hands pause over the chessboard (their weekly game is in progress) and he intones a verse from the Vedas:

From the Infinite, take the Infinite, and lo! Infinity remains . . .

Abdul Karim is astounded. That his ancestors could anticipate Georg Cantor by four millennia!

That fondness for science, . . . that affability and condescension which God shows to the learned, that promptitude with which he protects and supports them in the elucidation of obscurities and in the removal of difficulties, has encouraged me to compose a short work on calculating by al-jabr *and* al-muqabala, *confining it to what is easiest and most useful in arithmetic.*

—Al Khwarizmi, eighth century Arab mathematician

Mathematics came to the boy almost as naturally as breathing. He made a clean sweep of the exams in the little municipal school. The neighborhood was provincial, dominated by small tradesmen, minor government officials and the like, and their children seemed to have inherited or acquired their plodding practicality. Nobody understood that strangely clever Muslim boy, except for a Hindu classmate, Gangadhar, who was a well-liked, outgoing fellow. Although Gangadhar played gulli-danda on the streets and could run faster than anybody, he had a passion for literature, especially poetry—a pursuit perhaps as impractical as pure mathematics. The two were drawn together and spent many hours sitting on the compound wall at the back of the school, eating stolen jamuns from the trees overhead and talking about subjects ranging from Urdu poetry and Sanskrit verse to whether mathematics pervaded everything, including human emotions. They felt very grown-up and mature for their stations. Gangadhar was the one who, shyly, and with many giggles, first introduced Kalidasa's erotic poetry to Abdul Karim. At that time girls were a mystery to them both: although they shared classrooms it seemed to them that girls (a completely different species from their sisters, of course) were strange, graceful, alien creatures from another world. Kalidasa's lyrical descriptions of breasts and hips evoked in them unarticulated longings.

They had the occasional fight, as friends do. The first serious one happened when there were some Hindu-Muslim tensions in the city just before the elections. Gangadhar came to Abdul in the school playground and knocked him flat.

"You're a bloodthirsty Muslim!" he said, almost as though he had just realized it.

"You're a hell-bound kafir!"

They punched each other, wrestled the other to the ground. Finally, with cut lips and bruises, they stared fiercely at each other and staggered away. The next day they played gulli-danda in the street on opposite sides for the first time.

Then they ran into each other in the school library. Abdul Karim tensed, ready to hit back if Gangadhar hit him. Gangadhar looked as if he was thinking about it for a moment, but then, somewhat embarrassedly, he held out a book.

"New book . . . on mathematics. Thought you'd want to see it . . . "

After that they were sitting on the wall again, as usual.

Their friendship had even survived the great riots four years later, when the city became a charnel house—buildings and bodies burned, and unspeakable atrocities were committed by both Hindus and Muslims. Some political leader of one side or another had made a provocative proclamation that he could not even remember, and tempers had been inflamed. There was an incident—a fight at a bus-stop, accusations of police brutality against the Muslim side, and things had spiraled out of control. Abdul's elder sister Ayesha had been at the market with a cousin when the worst of the violence broke out. They had been separated in the stampede; the cousin had come back, bloodied but alive, and nobody had ever seen Ayesha again.

The family never recovered. Abdul's mother went through the motions of living but her heart wasn't in it. His father lost weight, became a shrunken mockery of his old, vigorous self—he would die only a few years later. As for Abdul—the news reports about atrocities fed his nightmares and in his dreams he saw his sister bludgeoned, raped, torn to pieces again and again and again. When the city calmed down, he spent his days roaming the streets of the market, hoping for a sign of Ayesha—a body even—torn between hope and feverish rage.

Their father stopped seeing his Hindu friends. The only reason Abdul did not follow suit was because Gangadhar's people had sheltered a Muslim family during the carnage, and had turned off a mob of enraged Hindus.

Over time the wound—if it did not quite heal—became bearable enough that he could start living again. He threw himself into his beloved mathematics, isolating himself from everyone but his family and Gangadhar. The world had wronged him. He did not owe it anything.

Aryabhata is the master who, after reaching the furthest shores and plumbing the inmost depths of the sea of ultimate knowledge of mathematics, kinematics and spherics, handed over the three sciences to the learned world.

—The Mathematician Bhaskara, commenting on the 6th century Indian mathematician Aryabhata, a hundred years later.

Abdul Karim was the first in his family to go to college. By a stroke of great luck, Gangadhar went to the same regional institution, majoring in Hindi literature while Abdul Karim buried himself in mathematical arcana. Abdul's father had become reconciled to his son's obsession and obvious talent. Abdul Karim himself, glowing with praise from his teachers, wanted to follow in the footsteps of Ramanujan. Just as the goddess Namakkal had appeared to that untutored genius in his dreams, writing mathematical formulas on his tongue (or so Ramanujan had said), Abdul Karim wondered if the farishte had been sent by Allah so that he, too, might be blessed with mathematical insight.

During that time an event occurred that convinced him of this.

Abdul was in the college library, working on a problem in differential geometry, when he sensed a farishta at the edge of his field of vision. As he had done countless times before, he turned his head slowly, expecting the vision to vanish.

Instead he saw a dark shadow standing in front of the long bookcase. It was vaguely human-shaped. It turned slowly, revealing itself to be thin as paper—but as it turned it seemed to acquire thickness, hints of features over its dark, slender form. And then it seemed to Abdul that a door opened in the air, just a crack, and he had a vision of an unutterably strange world beyond. The shadow stood at the door, beckoning with one arm, but Abdul Karim sat still, frozen with wonder. Before he could rouse himself and get up, the door and the shadow both rotated swiftly and vanished, and he was left staring at the stack of books on the shelf.

After this he was convinced of his destiny. He dreamed obsessively of the strange world he had glimpsed; every time he sensed a farishta he turned his head slowly toward it—and every time it vanished. He told himself it was just a matter of time before one of them came, remained, and perhaps—wonder of wonders—took him to that other world.

Then his father died unexpectedly. That was the end of Abdul Karim's career as a mathematician. He had to return home to take care of his mother, his two remaining sisters and a brother. The only thing he was qualified for was teaching. Ultimately he would find a job at the same municipal school from which he had graduated.

On the train home, he saw a woman. The train was stopped on a bridge. Below him was the sleepy curve of a small river, gold in the early morning light, mists rising faintly off it, and on the shore a woman with a clay water pot. She had taken a dip in the river—her pale, ragged sari clung wetly to her as she picked up the pot and set it on her hip and began to climb the bank. In the light of dawn she was luminous, an apparition in the mist, the curve of the pot against the curve of her hip. Their eyes met from a distance—he imagined what he thought she saw, the silent train, a young man with a sparse beard looking at her as though she was the first woman in the world. Her own eyes gazed at him fearlessly as though she were a goddess looking into his soul. For a moment there were no barriers between them, no boundaries of gender, religion, caste or class. Then she turned and vanished behind a stand of shisham trees.

He wasn't sure if she had really been there in the half-light or whether he had conjured her up, but for a long time she represented something elemental to him. Sometimes he thought of her as Woman, sometimes as a river.

He got home in time for the funeral. His job kept him busy, and kept the moneylender from their door. With the stubborn optimism of the young, he kept hoping that one day his fortunes would change, that he would go back to college and complete his degree. In the meantime, he knew his mother wanted to find him a bride . . .

Abdul Karim got married, had children. Slowly, over the years of managing rowdy classrooms, tutoring students in the afternoons and saving, paisa by paisa, from his meager salary for his sisters' weddings and other expenses, Abdul Karim lost touch with that youthful, fiery talent he had once had, and with it the ambition to scale the heights to which Ramanujan, Cantor and Riemann had climbed. Things came more slowly to him now. An intellect burdened by years of worry wears out. When his wife died and his children grew up and went away, his steadily decreasing needs finally caught up with his meager income, and he found for the first time that he could think about mathematics again. He no longer hoped to dazzle the world of mathematics with some new insight, such as a proof of Riemann's hypothesis. Those dreams were gone. All he could hope for was to be illumined by the efforts of those who had gone before him, and to re-live, vicariously, the joys of insight. It was a cruel trick of Time, that when he had the leisure he had lost the ability, but that is no bar to true obsession. Now, in the autumn of his life it was as though Spring had come again, bringing with it his old love.

In this world, brought to its knees by hunger and thirst
Love is not the only reality, there are other Truths . . .

—Sahir Ludhianvi, Indian poet (1921-1980)

There are times when Abdul Karim tires of his mathematical obsessions. After all, he is old. Sitting in the courtyard with his notebook, pencil and books of mathematics for so many hours at a stretch can take its toll. He gets up, aching all over, sees to his mother's needs and goes out to the graveyard where his wife is buried.

His wife Zainab had been a plump, fair-skinned woman, hardly able to read or write, who moved about the house with indolent grace, her good-natured laugh ringing out in the courtyard as she chattered with the washerwoman. She had loved to eat—he still remembered the delicate tips of her plump fingers, how they would curl around a piece of lamb, scooping up with it a few grains of saffron rice, the morsel conveyed reverently to her mouth. Her girth gave an impression of strength, but ultimately she had not been able to hold out against her mother-in-law. The laughter in her eyes faded gradually as her two boys grew out of babyhood, coddled and put to bed by the grandmother in her own corner of the women's quarters. Abdul Karim himself had been unaware of the silent war between his wife and mother—he had been young and obsessed with teaching mathematics to his recalcitrant students. He had noticed how the grandmother always seemed to be holding the younger son, crooning to him, and how the elder boy followed his mother around, but he did not see in this any connection to his wife's growing pallor. One night he had requested her to come to him and massage his feet—their euphemism for sex—and he had waited for her to come to him from the women's quarters, impatient for the comfort of her plump nakedness, her soft, silken breasts. When she came at last she had knelt at the foot of the bed, her chest heaving with muffled sobs, her hands covering her face. As he took her in his arms, wondering what could have ruffled her calm good nature, she had collapsed completely against him. No comfort he could offer would make her tell what it was that was breaking her heart. At last she begged him, between great, shuddering breaths, that all she wanted in the world was another baby.

Abdul Karim had been influenced by modern ideas—he considered two children, boys at that, to be quite sufficient for a family. As one of five children, he had known poverty and the pain of giving up his dream of a university career to help support his family. He wasn't going to have his children go through the same thing. But when his wife whispered to him that she wanted one more, he relented.

Now, when he looked back, he wished he had tried to understand the real reason for her distress. The pregnancy had been a troublesome one. His mother had taken charge of both boys almost entirely while Zainab lay in bed in the women's quarters, too sick to do anything but weep silently and call upon Allah to rescue her. "It's a girl," Abdul Karim's mother had said grimly. "Only a girl would cause so much trouble." She had looked away out of the window into the courtyard, where her own daughter, Abdul Karim's dead sister, Ayesha, had once played and helped hang the wash.

And finally it had been a girl, stillborn, who had taken her mother with her. They were buried together in the small, unkempt graveyard where Abdul Karim went whenever he was depressed. By now the gravestone was awry and grass had grown over the mound. His father was buried here also, and three of his siblings who had died before he was six. Only Ayesha, lost Ayesha, the one he remembered as a source of comfort to a small boy—strong, generous arms, hands delicate and fragrant with henna, a smooth cheek—she was not here.

In the graveyard Abdul Karim pays his respects to his wife's memory while his heart quails at the way the graveyard itself is disintegrating. He is afraid that if it goes to rack and ruin, overcome by vegetation and time, he will forget Zainab and the child and his guilt. Sometimes he tries to clear the weeds and tall grasses with his hands, but his delicate scholar's hands become bruised and sore quite quickly, and he sighs and thinks about the Sufi poetess Jahanara, who had written, centuries earlier: "Let the green grass grow above my grave!"

I have often pondered over the roles of knowledge or experience, on the one hand, and imagination or intuition, on the other, in the process of discovery. I believe that there is a certain fundamental conflict between the two, and knowledge, by advocating caution, tends to inhibit the flight of imagination. Therefore, a certain naivete, unburdened by conventional wisdom, can sometimes be a positive asset.

—Harish-Chandra, Indian mathematician (1923-1983).

Gangadhar, his friend from school, was briefly a master of Hindi literature at the municipal school and is now an academician at the Amravati Heritage Library, and a poet in his spare time. He is the only person to whom Abdul Karim can confide his secret passion.

In time, he too becomes intrigued with the idea of infinity. While Abdul Karim pores over Cantor and Riemann, and tries to make meaning from the Prime Number theorem, Gangadhar raids the library and brings forth treasures. Every week, when Abdul Karim walks the two miles to Gangadhar's house, where he is led by the servant to the comfortable drawing room with its gracious, if aging mahogany furniture, the two men share what they've learned over cups of cardamom tea and a chess game. Gangadhar cannot understand higher mathematics but he can sympathize with the frustrations of the knowledge-seeker, and he has known what it is like to chip away at the wall of ignorance and burst into the light of understanding. He digs out quotes from Aryabhata and Al-Khwarizmi, and tells his friend such things as:

"Did you know, Abdul, that the Greeks and Romans did not like the idea of infinity? Aristotle argued against it, and proposed a finite universe. Of the yunaanis, only Archimedes dared to attempt to scale that peak. He came up with the notion that different infinite quantities could be compared, that one infinite could be greater or smaller than another infinite . . . "

And on another occasion:

"The French mathematician, Jacques Hadamard . . . He was the one who proved the Prime Number theorem that has you in such ecstasies . . . he says there are four stages to mathematical discovery. Not very different from the experience of the artist or poet, if you think about it. The first is to study and be familiar with what is known. The next is to let these ideas turn in your mind, as the earth regenerates by lying fallow between plantings. Then—with luck—there is the flash of insight, the illuminating moment when you discover something new and feel in your bones that it must be true. The final stage is to verify—to subject that epiphany to the rigors of mathematical proof . . . "

Abdul Karim feels that if he can simply go through Hadamard's first two stages, perhaps Allah will reward him with a flash of insight. And perhaps not. If he had hopes of being another Ramanujan, those hopes are gone now. But no true Lover has ever turned from the threshold of the Beloved's house, even knowing he will not be admitted through the doors.

"What worries me," he confides to Gangadhar during one of these discussions, "what has always worried me, is Gödel's Incompleteness Theorem. According to Gödel, there can be statements in mathematics that are not provable. He showed that the Continuum Hypothesis of Cantor was one of these statements. Poor Cantor, he lost his sanity trying to prove something that cannot be proved or disproved! What if all our unproven ideas on prime numbers, on infinity, are statements like that? If they can't be tested against the constraints of mathematical logic, how will we ever know if they are true?"

This bothers him very much. He pores over the proof of Gödel's theorem, seeking to understand it, to get around it. Gangadhar encourages him:

"You know, in the old tales, every great treasure is guarded by a proportionally great monster. Perhaps Gödel's theorem is the djinn that guards the truth you seek. Maybe instead of slaying it, you have to, you know, befriend it . . . "

Through his own studies, through discussions with Gangadhar, Abdul Karim begins to feel again that his true companions are Archimedes, Al-Khwarizmi. Khayyam, Aryabhata, Bhaskar. Riemann, Cantor, Gauss, Ramanujan, Hardy.

They are the masters, before whom he is as a humble student, an apprentice following their footprints up the mountainside. The going is rough. He is getting old, after all. He gives himself up to dreams of mathematics, rousing himself only to look after the needs of his mother, who is growing more and more frail.

After a while, even Gangadhar admonishes him.

"A man cannot live like this, so obsessed. Will you let yourself go the way of Cantor and Gödel? Guard your sanity, my friend. You have a duty to your mother, to society."

Abdul Karim cannot make Gangadhar understand. His mind sings with mathematics.

The limit of a function f(N) as N goes to infinity . . . ..

So many questions he asks himself begin like this. The function f(N) may be the prime counting function, or the number of nested dolls of matter, or the extent of the universe. It may be abstract, like a parameter in a mathematical space, or earthy, like the branching of wrinkles in the face of his mother, growing older and older in the paved courtyard of his house, under the litchi trees. Older and older, without quite dying, as though she were determined to live Zeno's paradox.

He loves his mother the way he loves the litchi tree; for being there, for making him what he is, for giving him shelter and succor.

The limit . . . as N goes to infinity . . .

So begin many theorems of calculus. Abdul Karim wonders what kind of calculus governs his mother's slow arc into dying. What if life did not require a minimum threshold of conditions—what if death were merely a limit of some function f(N) as N goes to infinity?

A world in which human life is but a pawn
A world filled with death-worshipers,
Where death is cheaper than life . . .
That world is not my world . . .

—Sahir Ludhianvi, Indian poet (1921-1980)

While Abdul Karim dabbles in the mathematics of the infinite, as so many deluded fools and geniuses have done, the world changes.

He is vaguely aware that there are things going on in the world— that people live and die, that there are political upheavals, that this is the hottest summer yet and already a thousand people have died of the heat wave in Northern India. He knows that Death also stands at his mother's shoulder, waiting, and he does what he can for her. Although he has not always observed the five daily prayers, he does the namaz now, with her. She has already started becoming the citizen of another country—she lives in little leaps and bends of time long gone, calling for Ayesha one moment, and for her long-dead husband the next. Conversations from her lost girlhood emerge from her trembling mouth. In her few moments of clarity she calls upon Allah to take her away.

Dutiful as he is to his mother, Abdul Karim is relieved to be able to get away once a week for a chess game and conversation with Gangadhar. He has a neighbor's aunt look in on his mother during that time. Heaving a sigh or two, he makes his way through the familiar lanes of his childhood, his shoes scuffing up dust under the ancient jamun trees that he once climbed as a child. He greets his neighbors: old Ameen Khan Sahib sitting on his charpai, wheezing over his hookah, the Ali twins, madcap boys chasing a bicycle tire with a stick, Imran at the paan shop. He crosses, with some trepidation, the increasingly congested market road, past the faded awnings of Munshilal and Sons, past a rickshaw stand into another quiet lane, this one shaded with jacaranda trees. Gangadhar's house is a modest white bungalow, stained an indeterminate gray from many monsoons. The creak of the wooden gate in the compound wall is as familiar a greeting as Gangadhar's welcome.

But the day comes when there is no chess game at Gangadhar's house.

The servant boy—not Gangadhar—ushers him into the familiar room. Sitting down in his usual chair, Abdul Karim notices that the chess board has not been laid out. Sounds come from the inner rooms of the house: women's voices, heavy objects being dragged across the floor.

An elderly man comes into the room and stops short as though surprised to see Abdul Karim. He looks vaguely familiar—then Abdul remembers that he is some relative of Gangadhar's wife—an uncle, perhaps—and he lives on the other side of the city. They have met once or twice at some family celebration.

"What are you doing here?" the man says, without any of the usual courtesies. He is white-haired but of vigorous build.

Puzzled and a little affronted, Abdul Karim says:

"I am here for my chess game with Gangadhar. Is he not at home?"

"There will be no chess game today. Haven't you people done enough harm? Are you here to mock us in our sorrow? Well, let me tell you . . . "

"What happened?" Abdul Karim's indignation is dissolving in a wave of apprehension. "What are you talking about? Is Gangadhar all right?"

"Perhaps you don't know," says the man, his tone mocking. "Some of your people burned a bus on Paharia road yesterday evening. There were ten people on it, all Hindus, coming back from a family ceremony at a temple. They all perished horribly. Word has it that you people did it. Didn't even let the children get off the bus. Now the whole town is in turmoil. Who knows what might happen? Gangadhar and I are taking his family to a safer part of town."

Abdul Karim's eyes are wide with shock. He can find no words.

"All these hundreds of years we Hindus have tolerated you people. Even though you Muslims raided and pillaged us over the centuries, we let you build your mosques, worship your God. And this is how you pay us!"

In one instant Abdul Karim has become "you people." He wants to say that he did not lift an arm to hurt those who perished on the bus. His were not the hands that set the fire. But no words come out.

"Can you imagine it, Master Sahib? Can you see the flames? Hear their screams? Those people will never go home . . . "

"I can imagine it," Abdul Karim says, grimly now. He rises to his feet, but just then Gangadhar enters the room. He has surely heard part of the conversation because he puts his hands on Abdul Karim's shoulders, gently, recognizing him as the other man has not done. This is Abdul Karim, his friend, whose sister, all those years ago, never came home.

Gangadhar turns to his wife's uncle.

"Uncle, please. Abdul Karim is not like those miscreants. A kinder man I have never known! And as yet it is not known who the ruffians are, although the whole town is filled with rumors. Abdul, please sit down! This is a measure of the times we live in, that we can say such things to each other. Alas! Kalyug is indeed upon us."

Abdul Karim sits down, but he is shaking. All thoughts of mathematics have vanished from his mind. He is filled with disgust and revulsion for the barbarians who committed this atrocity, for human beings in general. What a degraded species we are! To take the name of Ram or Allah, or Jesus, and to burn and destroy under one aegis or another—that is what our history has been.

The uncle, shaking his head, has left the room. Gangadhar is talking history to Abdul, apologizing for his uncle.

" . . . a matter of political manipulation," he says. "The British colonialists looked for our weakness, exploited it, set us against each other. Opening the door to hell is easy enough—but closing it is hard. All those years, before British rule, we lived in relative peace. Why is it that we cannot close that door they opened? After all, what religion tells us to slay our neighbor?"

"Does it matter?" Abdul Karim says bitterly. "We humans are a depraved species, my friend. My fellow Muslims address every prayer to Allah, the Merciful and Compassionate. You Hindus, with your "Isha Vasyam Idam Sarvam"—the divine pervades all. The Christians talk on about turning the other cheek. And yet each of them has hands that are stained in blood. We pervert everything—we take the words of peace spoken by prophets and holy men and turn them into weapons with which to kill each other!"

He is shaking so hard that he can barely speak.

"It is in mathematics . . . only in mathematics that I see Allah . . . "

"Quiet now," Gangadhar says. He calls for the servant to bring some water for the master sahib. Abdul Karim drinks and wipes his mouth. The suitcases are being brought out from inside the house. There is a taxi in front.

"Listen, my friend," Gangadhar says, "you must look to your safety. Go home now and lock your doors, and look after your mother. I am sending my family away and I will join them in a day or so. When this madness has passed I will come and look for you!"

Abdul Karim goes home. So far everything looks normal—the wind is blowing litter along in the streets, the paan shop is open, people throng the bus-stop. Then he notices that there aren't any children, even though the summer holidays are going on.

The vegetable market is very busy. People are buying up everything like crazy. He buys a few potatoes, onions and a large gourd, and goes home. He locks the door. His mother, no longer up to cooking meals, watches as he cooks. After they eat and he has her tucked into bed, he goes to his study and opens a book on mathematics.

One day passes, perhaps two—he does not keep track. He remembers to take care of his mother but often forgets to eat. His mother lives, more and more, in that other world. His sisters and brother call from other towns, anxious about the reports of escalating violence; he tells them not to worry. When things are back to normal they will come and see him and their mother.

How marvelous, the Universal Mystery
That only a true Lover can comprehend!

—Bulleh Shah, eighteenth century Punjabi Sufi poet

Logic merely sanctions the conquests of the intuition.

—Jacques Hadamard, French mathematician (1865-1963)

One morning he emerges from the darkness of his study into the sunny courtyard. Around him the old city writhes and burns, but Abdul Karim sees and hears nothing but mathematics. He sits in his old cane chair, picks up a stick lying on the ground and begins to draw mathematical symbols in the dust.

There is a farishta standing at the edge of his vision.

He turns slowly. The dark shadow stays there, waits. This time Abdul Karim is quick on his feet, despite a sudden twinge of pain in one knee. He walks toward the door, the beckoning arm, and steps through.

For a moment he is violently disoriented—it occurs to him that he has spun through a different dimension into this hidden world. Then the darkness before his eyes dissipates, and he beholds wonders.

All is hushed. He is looking at a vast sweep of land and sky unlike anything he has ever seen. Dark, pyramidal shapes stud the landscape, great monuments to something beyond his understanding. There is a vast, polyhedral object suspended in a pale orange sky that has no sun. Only a diffuse luminescence pervades this sky. He looks at his feet, still in his familiar, worn sandals, and sees all around, in the sand, little fish-like creatures wriggling and spawning. Some of the sand has worked its way between his toes, and it feels warm and rubbery, not like sand at all. He takes a deep breath and smells something strange, like burnt rubber mixed with his own sweat. The shadow stands by his side, looking solid at last, almost human but for the absence of neck and the profusion of limbs—their number seems to vary with time—at the moment Abdul Karim counts five.

The dark orifice in the head opens and closes, but no sound comes out. Instead Abdul feels as though a thought has been placed in his mind, a package that he will open later.

He walks with the shadow across the sands to the edge of a quiet sea. The water, if that is what it is, is foaming and bubbling gently, and within its depths he sees ghostly shapes moving, and the hints of complex structure far below. Arabesques form in the depths, break up, and form again. He licks his dry lips, tastes metal and salt.

He looks at his companion, who bids him pause. A door opens. They step through into another universe.

It is different, this one. It is all air and light, the whole space hung with great, translucent webbing. Each strand in the web is a hollow tube within which liquid creatures flow. Smaller, solid beings float in the emptiness between the web strands.

Speechless, he stretches out his hand toward a web-strand. Its delicacy reminds him of the filigreed silver anklets his wife used to wear. To his complete surprise a tiny being floating within the strand stops. It is like a plump, watery comma, translucent and without any features he can recognize, and yet he has the notion that he is being looked at, examined, and that at the other end is also wonder.

The web-strand touches him, and he feels its cool, alien smoothness on a fingertip.

A door opens. They step through.

It is dizzying, this wild ride. Sometimes he gets flashes of his own world, scenes of trees and streets, and distant blue hills. There are indications that these flashes are at different points in time—at one point he sees a vast army of soldiers, their plumed helmets catching the sunlight, and thinks he must be in the time of the Roman Empire. Another time he thinks he is back home, because he sees before him his own courtyard. But there is an old man sitting in his cane chair, drawing patterns in the dust with a stick. A shadow falls across the ground. Someone he cannot see is stealing up behind the old man. Is that a knife agleam in the stranger's hand? What is this he is seeing? He tries to call out, but no sound emerges. The scene blurs—a door opens, and they step through.

Abdul Karim is trembling. Has he just witnessed his own death?

He remembers that Archimedes died that way—he had been drawing circles, engrossed with a problem in geometry, when a barbarian of a soldier came up behind him and killed him.

But there is no time to ponder. He is lost in a merry-go-round of universes, each different and strange. The shadow gives him a glimpse of so many, Abdul Karim has long lost count. He puts thoughts of Death away from him and loses himself in wonder.

His companion opens door after door. The face, featureless except for the orifice that opens and shuts, gives no hint of what the shadow is thinking. Abdul Karim wants to ask: who are you? Why are you doing this? He knows, of course, the old story of how the angel Gabriel came to the Prophet Mohammad one night and took him on a celestial journey, a grand tour of the heavens. But the shadow does not look like an angel; it has no face, no wings, its gender is indeterminate. And in any case, why should the angel Gabriel concern himself with a humble mathematics master in a provincial town, a person of no consequence in the world?

And yet, he is here. Perhaps Allah has a message for him; His ways are ineffable, after all. Exultation fills Abdul Karim as he beholds marvel after marvel.

At last they pause in a place where they are suspended in a yellow sky. As Abdul Karim experiences the giddy absence of gravity, accompanied by a sudden jolt of nausea that slowly recedes—as he turns in mid-air, he notices that the sky is not featureless but covered with delicate tessellations: geometric shapes intertwine, merge and new ones emerge. The colors change too, from yellow to green, lilac, mauve. All at once it seems as though numberless eyes are opening in the sky, one after the other, and as he turns he sees all the other universes flashing past him. A kaleidoscope, vast beyond his imaginings. He is at the center of it all, in a space between all spaces, and he can feel in his bones a low, irregular throbbing, like the beating of a drum. Boom, boom, goes the drum. Boom boom boom. Slowly he realizes that what he is seeing and feeling is part of a vast pattern.

In that moment Abdul Karim has the flash of understanding he has been waiting for all his life.

For so long he has been playing with the transcendental numbers, trying to fathom Cantor's ideas; at the same time Riemann's notions of the prime numbers have fascinated him. In idle moments he has wondered if they are connected at a deeper level. Despite their apparent randomness the primes have their own regularity, as hinted by the unproven Riemann Hypothesis; he sees at last that if you think of prime numbers as the terrain of a vast country, and if your view of reality is a two-dimensional plane that intersects this terrain at some height above the surface, perhaps at an angle, then of course what you see will appear to be random. Tops of hills. Bits of valleys. Only the parts of the terrain that cross your plane of reality will be apparent. Unless you can see the entire landscape in its multi-dimensional splendor, the topography will make no sense.

He sees it: the bare bones of creation, here, in this place where all the universes branch off, the thudding heart of the metacosmos. In the scaffolding, the skeletal structure of the multiverse is beautifully apparent. This is what Cantor had a glimpse of, then, this vast topography. Understanding opens in his mind as though the metacosmos has itself spoken to him. He sees that of all the transcendental numbers, only a few—infinite still, but not the whole set—are marked as doorways to other universes, and each is labeled by a prime number. Yes. Yes. Why this is so, what deeper symmetry it reflects, what law or regularity of Nature undreamed of by the physicists of his world, he does not know.

The space where primes live—the topology of the infinite universes— he sees it in that moment. No puny function as yet dreamed of by humans can encompass the vastness—the inexhaustible beauty of this place. He knows that he can never describe this in the familiar symbols of the mathematics that he knows, that while he experiences the truth of the Riemann Hypothesis, as a corollary to this greater, more luminous reality, he cannot sit down and verify it through a conventional proof. No human language as yet exists, mathematical or otherwise, that can describe what he knows in his bones to be true. Perhaps he, Abdul

Karim, will invent the beginnings of such a language. Hadn't the great poet Iqbal interpreted the Prophet's celestial journey to mean that the heavens are within our grasp?

A twist, and a door opens. He steps into the courtyard of his house. He turns around, but the courtyard is empty. The farishta is gone.

Abdul Karim raises his eyes to the heavens. Rain clouds, dark as the proverbial beloved's hair, sweep across the sky; the litchi tree over his head is dancing in the swift breeze. The wind has drowned out the sounds of a ravaged city. A red flower comes blowing over the courtyard wall and is deposited at his feet.

Abdul Karim's hair is blown back, a nameless ecstasy fills him; he feels Allah's breath on his face.

He says into the wind:

Dear Merciful and Compassionate God, I stand before your wondrous universe, filled with awe; help me, weak mortal that I am, to raise my gaze above the sordid pettiness of everyday life, the struggles and quarrels of mean humanity . . . Help me to see the beauty of your Works, from the full flower of the red silk cotton tree to the exquisite mathematical grace by which you have created numberless universes in the space of a man's step. I know now that my true purpose in this sad world is to stand in humble awe before your magnificence, and to sing a paean of praise to you with every breath I take . . .

He feels weak with joy. Leaves whirl in the courtyard like mad dervishes; a drop or two of rain falls, obliterating the equation he had scratched in the dust with his stick. He has lost his chance at mathematical genius a long time ago; he is nobody, only a teacher of mathematics at a school, humbler than a clerk in a government office—yet Allah has favored him with this great insight. Perhaps he is now worthy of speech with Ramanujan and Archimedes and all the ones in between. But all he wants to do is to run out into the lane and go shouting through the city: see, my friends, open your eyes and see what I see! But he knows they would think him mad; only Gangadhar would understand . . . if not the mathematics then the impulse, the importance of the whole discovery.

He leaps out of the house, into the lane.

This blemished radiance . . . this night-stung dawn
Is not the dawn we waited for . . .

—Faiz Ahmed Faiz, Pakistani poet (1911-1984)

Where all is broken
Where each soul's athirst, each glance
Filled with confusion, each heart
Weighed with sorrow . . .
Is this a world, or chaos?

—Sahir Ludhianvi, Indian poet (1921-1980)

But what is this? The lane is empty. There are broken bottles everywhere. The windows and doors of his neighbors' houses are shuttered and barred, like closed eyes. Above the sound of the rain he hears shouting in the distance. Why is there a smell of burning?

He remembers then, what he had learned at Gangadhar's house. Securing the door behind him, he begins to run as fast as his old-man legs will carry him.

The market is burning.

Smoke pours out of smashed store fronts, even as the rain falls. There is broken glass on the pavement; a child's wooden doll in the middle of the road, decapitated. Soggy pages filled with neat columns of figures lie scattered everywhere, the remains of a ledger. Quickly he crosses the road.

Gangadhar's house is in ruins. Abdul Karim wanders through the open doors, stares blindly at the blackened walls. The furniture is mostly gone. Only the chess table stands untouched in the middle of the front room.

Frantically he searches through the house, entering the inner rooms for the first time. Even the curtains have been ripped from the windows.

There is no body.

He runs out of the house. Gangadhar's wife's family—he does not know where they live. How to find out if Gangadhar is safe?

The neighboring house belongs to a Muslim family that Abdul Karim knows only from visits to the mosque. He pounds on the door. He thinks he hears movement behind the door, sees the upstairs curtains twitch—but nobody answers his frantic entreaties. At last, defeated, his hands bleeding, he walks slowly home, looking about him in horror. Is this truly his city, his world?

Allah, Allah, why have you abandoned me?

He has beheld the glory of Allah's workmanship. Then why this? Were all those other universes, other realities a dream?

The rain pours down.

There is someone lying on his face in a ditch. The rain has wet the shirt on his back, made the blood run. As Abdul Karim starts toward him, wondering who it is, whether he is dead or alive—young, from the back it could be Ramdas or Imran—he sees behind him, at the entrance to the lane, a horde of young men. Some of them may be his students—they can help.

They are moving with a predatory sureness that frightens him. He sees that they have sticks and stones.

They are coming like a tsunami, a thunderclap, leaving death and ruin in their wake. He hears their shouts through the rain.

Abdul Karim's courage fails him. He runs to his house, enters, locks and bars the door and closes all the windows. He checks on his mother, who is sleeping. The telephone is dead. The dal for their meal has boiled away. He turns off the gas and goes back to the door, putting his ear against it. He does not want to risk looking out of the window.

Over the rain he hears the young men go past at a run. In the distance there is a fusillade of shots. More sounds of running feet, then, just the rain.

Are the police here? The army?

Something or someone is scratching at the door. Abdul Karim is transfixed with terror. He stands there, straining to hear over the pitter patter of the rain. On the other side, somebody moans.

Abdul Karim opens the door. The lane is empty, roaring with rain. At his feet there is the body of a young woman.

She opens her eyes. She's dressed in a salwaar kameez that has been half-torn off her body—her long hair is wet with rain and blood, plastered over her neck and shoulders. There is blood on her salwaar, blood oozing from a hundred little cuts and welts on her skin.

Her gaze focuses.

"Master Sahib.."

He is taken aback. Is she someone he knows? Perhaps an old student, grown up?

Quickly he half-carries, half-pulls her into the house and secures the door. With some difficulty he lifts her carefully on to the divan in the drawing room, which is already staining with her blood. She coughs.

"My child, who did this to you? Let me find a doctor . . . "

"No," she says. "It's too late." Her breath rasps and she coughs again. Tears well up in the dark eyes.

"Master Sahib, please, let me die! My husband . . . my son . . . They must not see me take my last breath. Not like this. They will suffer. They will want revenge . . . Please . . . cut my wrists . . . "

She's raising her wrists to his horrified face, but all he can do is to take them in his shaking hands.

"My daughter," he says, and doesn't know what to say. Where will he find a doctor in the mayhem? Can he bind her cuts? Even as he thinks these thoughts he knows that life is ebbing from her. Blood is pooling on his divan, dripping down to the floor. She does not need him to cut her wrists.

"Tell me, who are the ruffians who did this?"

She whispers:

"I don't know who they were. I had just stepped out of the house for a moment. My family . . . don't tell them, Master Sahib! When I'm gone just tell them . . . tell them I died in a safe place . . . "

"Daughter, what is your husband's name?"

Her eyes are enormous. She is gazing at him without comprehension, as though she is already in another world.

He can't tell if she is Muslim or Hindu. If she wore a vermilion dot on her forehead, it has long since been washed off by the rain.

His mother is standing at the door of the drawing room. She wails suddenly and loudly, flings herself by the side of the dying woman.

"Ayesha! Ayesha, my life!"

Tears fall down Abdul Karim's face. He tries to disengage his mother. Tries to tell her: this is not Ayesha, just another woman whose body has become a battleground over which men make war. At last he has to lift his mother in his arms, her body so frail that he fears it might break—he takes her to her bed, where she crumples, sobbing and calling Ayesha's name.

Back in the drawing room, the young woman's eyes flicker to him. Her voice is barely above a whisper.

"Master Sahib, cut my wrists . . . I beseech you, in the Almighty's name! Take me somewhere safe . . . Let me die . . . "

Then the veil falls over her eyes again and her body goes limp.

Time stands still for Abdul Karim.

Then he senses something familiar, and turns slowly. The farishta is waiting.

Abdul Karim picks up the woman in his arms, awkwardly arranging the bloody divan cover over her half-naked body. In the air, a door opens.

Staggering a little, his knees protesting, he steps through the door.

After three universes he finds the place.

It is peaceful. There is a rock rising from a great turquoise sea of sand. The blue sand laps against the rock, making lulling, sibilant sounds. In the high, clear air, winged creatures call to each other between endless rays of light. He squints in the sudden brightness.

He closes her eyes, buries her deep at the base of the rock, under the blue, flowing sand.

He stands there, breathing hard from the exertion, his hands bruised, thinking he should say something. But what? He does not even know if she's Muslim or Hindu. When she spoke to him earlier, what word had she used for God? Was it Allah or Ishwar, or something neutral?

He can't remember.

At last he says the Al-Fatihah, and, stumbling a little, recites whatever little he knows of the Hindu scriptures. He ends with the phrase *Isha Vasyamidam Sarvam.*

Tears run off his cheeks into the blue sand, and disappear without leaving a trace.

The farishta waits.

"Why didn't you do something!" Abdul Karim rails at the shadow. He falls to his knees in the blue sand, weeping. "Why, if you are truly a farishta, didn't you save my sister?"

He sees now that he has been a fool—this shadow creature is no angel, and he, Abdul Karim, no Prophet.

He weeps for Ayesha, for this nameless young woman, for the body he saw in the ditch, for his lost friend Gangadhar.

The shadow leans toward him. Abdul Karim gets up, looks around once, and steps through the door.

He steps out into his drawing room. The first thing he discovers is that his mother is dead. She looks quite peaceful, lying in her bed, her white hair flowing over the pillow.

She might be asleep, her face is so calm.

He stands there for a long time, unable to weep. He picks up the phone—there is still no dial tone. After that he goes about methodically cleaning up the drawing room, washing the floor, taking the bedding off the divan. Later, after the rain has stopped, he will burn it in the courtyard. Who will notice another fire in the burning city?

When everything is cleaned up, he lies down next to his mother's body like a small boy and goes to sleep.

When you left me, my brother, you took away the book
In which is writ the story of my life . . .

—Faiz Ahmed Faiz, Pakistani poet (1911-1984)

The sun is out. An uneasy peace lies over the city. His mother's funeral is over. Relatives have come and gone—his younger son came, but did not stay. The older son sent a sympathy card from America.

Gangadhar's house is still empty, a blackened ruin. Whenever he has ventured out, Abdul Karim has asked about his friend's whereabouts. The last he heard was that Gangadhar was alone in the house when the mob came, and his Muslim neighbors sheltered him until he could join his wife and children at her parents' house. But it has been so long that he does not believe it any more. He has also heard that Gangadhar was dragged out, hacked to pieces and his body set on fire. The city has calmed down—the army had to be called in—but it is still rife with rumors. Hundreds of people are missing. Civil rights groups comb the town, interviewing people, revealing, in clipped, angry press statements, the negligence of the state government, the collusion of the police in some of the violence. Some of them came to his house, too, very clean, very young people, burning with an idealism that, however misplaced, is comforting to see. He has said nothing about the young woman who died in his arms, but he prays for that bereft family every day.

For days he has ignored the shadow at his shoulder. But now he knows that the sense of betrayal will fade. Whose fault is it, after all, that he ascribed to the creatures he once called farishte the attributes of angels? Could angels, even, save human beings from themselves?

The creatures watch us with a child's curiosity, he thinks, but they do not understand. Just as their own worlds are incomprehensible to me, so are our ways to them. They are not Allah's minions.

The space where the universes branch off—the heart of the metacosmos—now appears remote to him, like a dream. He is ashamed of his earlier arrogance. How can he possibly fathom Allah's creation in one glance? No finite mind can, in one meager lifetime, truly comprehend the vastness, the grandeur of Allah's scheme. All we can do is to discover a bit of the truth here, a bit there, and thus to sing His praises.

But there is so much pain in Abdul Karim's soul that he cannot imagine writing down one syllable of the new language of the infinite. His dreams are haunted by the horrors he has seen, the images of his mother and the young woman who died in his arms. He cannot even say his prayers. It is as though Allah has abandoned him, after all.

The daily task of living—waking up, performing his ablutions, setting the little pot on the gas stove to boil water for one cup of tea, to drink that tea alone—unbearable thought! To go on, after so many have died—to go on without his mother, his children, without Gangadhar . . . Everything appears strangely remote: his aging face in the mirror, the old house, even the litchi tree in his courtyard. The familiar lanes of his childhood hold memories that no longer seem to belong to him. Outside, the neighbors are in mourning; old Ameen Khan Sahib weeps for his grandson; Ramdas is gone, Imran is gone. The wind still carries the soot of the burnings. He finds little piles of ashes everywhere, in the cracks in the cement of his courtyard, between the roots of the trees in the lane. He breathes the dead. How can he regain his heart, living in a world so wracked with pain? In this world there is no place for the likes of him. No place for henna-scented hands rocking a child to sleep, for old-woman hands tending a garden. And no place at all for the austere beauty of mathematics.

He's thinking this when a shadow falls across the ground in front of him. He has been sitting in his courtyard, idly writing mathematical expressions with his stick on the dusty ground. He does not know whether the knife bearer is his son, or an enraged Hindu, but he finds himself ready for his death. The creatures who have watched him for so long will witness it, and wonder. Their uncomprehending presence comforts him.

He turns and rises. It is Gangadhar, his friend, who holds out his empty arms in an embrace.

Abdul Karim lets his tears run over Gangadhar's shirt. As waves of relief wash over him he knows that he has held Death at bay this time, but it will come. It will come, he has seen it. Archimedes and Ramanujan, Khayyam and Cantor died with epiphanies on their lips before an indifferent world. But this moment is eternal.

"Allah be praised!" says Abdul Karim.

First published in
Woman Who Thought She Was a Planet and Other Stories
by Vandana Singh, 2009.

ABOUT THE AUTHOR

Vandana Singh was born and raised in New Delhi, India. She acquired a passion for inventing her own myths around the age of eleven, and obtained a Ph.D. in theoretical particle physics in her twenties. She now teaches physics at a small state university near Boston, and obsesses over everything from human nature to climate change to creative pedagogies. Her short stories have appeared most recently in *The Other Half of the Sky* (ed. Athena Andreadis) and *Solaris Rising 2* (ed. Ian Whates), and several have been reprinted in best-of-year anthologies.

Martian Heart

JOHN BARNES

Okay, botterogator, I agreed to this. Now you're supposed to guide me to tell my story to *inspire a new generation of Martians.* It is so weird that there *is* a new generation of Martians. So hit me with the questions, or whatever it is you do.

Do I want to be *consistent with previous public statements?*

Well, every time they ask me where I got all the money and got to be such a big turd in the toilet that is Mars, I always say Samantha was my inspiration. So let's check that box for tentatively consistent.

Thinking about Sam always gives me weird thoughts. And here are two: one, before her, I would not have known what either *tentatively* or *consistent* even meant. Two, in these pictures, Samantha looks younger than my granddaughter is now.

So weird. She *was.*

We were in bed in our place under an old underpass in LA when the sweeps busted in, grabbed us up, and dragged us to the processing station. No good lying about whether we had family—they had our retinas and knew we were strays. Since I was seventeen and Sam was fifteen, they couldn't make any of our family pay for re-edj.

So they gave us fifteen minutes on the bench there to decide between twenty years in the forces, ten years in the glowies, or going out to Mars on this opposition and coming back on the third one after, in six and a half years.

They didn't tell you, and it wasn't well-known, that even people without the genetic defect suffered too much cardiac atrophy in that time to safely come back to Earth. The people that went to Mars didn't have family or friends to write back to, and the settlement program was so new it didn't seem strange that nobody knew a returned Martian.

"Crap," I said.

"Well, at least it's a future." Sam worried about the future a lot more than me. "If we enlist, there's no guarantee we'll be assigned together, unless we're married, and they don't let you get married till you've been in for three. We'd have to write each other letters—"

"Sam," I said, "I can't write to you or read your letters if you send me any. You know that."

"They'd make you learn."

I tried not to shudder visibly; she'd get mad if I let her see that I didn't really want to learn. "Also, that thing you always say about out of sight, that'd happen. I'd have another girlfriend in like, not long. I just would. I know we're all true love and everything but I would."

"The spirit is willing but the flesh is *more* willing." She always made those little jokes that only she got. "Okay, then, no forces for us."

"Screw glowies," I said. Back in those days right after the baby nukes had landed all over the place, the Decon Admin needed people to operate shovels, hoes, and detectors. I quoted this one hook from our favorite music. "*Sterile or dead or kids with three heads.*"

"And we *can* get married going to Mars," Sam said, "and then they *can't* separate us. True love forever, baby." Sam always had all the ideas.

So, botterogator, check that box for *putting a priority on family/love.* I guess since that new box popped up as soon as I said, *Sam always had all the ideas,* that means you want more about that? Yeah, now it's bright and bouncing. Okay, more about how she had all the ideas.

Really all the ideas I ever had were about eating, getting high, and scoring ass. Hunh. Red light. Guess that wasn't what you wanted for the new generation of Martians.

Sam was different. Everybody I knew was thinking about the next party or at most the next week or the next boy or girl, but Sam thought about *everything*. I know it's a stupid example, but once back in LA, she came into our squat and found me fucking with the fusion box, just to mess with it. "That supplies all our power for music, light, heat, net, and everything, and you can't fix it if you break it, and it's not broke, so, Cap, what the fuck are you doing?"

See, I didn't even have ideas *that* good.

So a year later, there on the bench, our getting married was her having another idea and me going along with it, which was always how things worked, when they worked. Ten minutes later we registered as married.

Orientation for Mars was ten days. The first day they gave us shots, bleached our tats into white blotches on our skin, and shaved our heads. They stuck us in ugly dumb coveralls and didn't let us have real clothes that said anything, which they said was so we wouldn't know who'd been what on Earth. I think it was more so we all looked like transportees.

The second day, and every day after, they tried to pound some knowledge into us. It was almost interesting. Sam was in with the people that could read, and she seemed to know more than I did afterward. Maybe there was something to that reading stuff, or it might also have been that freaky, powerful memory of hers.

Once we were erased and oriented, they loaded Sam and me into a two-person cube on a dumpround to Mars. Minutes after the booster released us and we were ballistic, an older guy, some asshole, tried to come into our cube and tell us this was going to be his space all to himself, and I punched him hard enough to take him out; I don't think he had his balance for centrifigrav yet.

Two of his buds jumped in. I got into it with them too—I was hot, they were pissing me off, I wasn't figuring odds. Then some guys from the cubes around me came in with me, and together we beat the other side's ass bloody.

In the middle of the victory whooping, Sam shouted for quiet. She announced, "Everyone stays in their same quarters. Everyone draws their own rations. Everyone takes your turn, and *just* your turn, at the info screens. And nobody doesn't pay for protection or nothing."

One of the assholes, harmless now because I had at least ten good guys at my back, sneered, "Hey, little bitch. You running for Transportee Council?"

"Sure, why not?"

She won, too.

The Transportee Council stayed in charge for the whole trip. People ate and slept in peace, and no crazy-asses broke into the server array, which is what caused most lost dumprounds. They told us in orientation, but a lot of transportees didn't listen, or didn't understand, or just didn't believe that a dumpround didn't have any fuel to go back to Earth; a dumpround flew like a cannon ball, with just a few little jets to guide it in and out of the aerobrakes and steer it to the parachute field.

The same people who thought there was a steering wheel in the server array compartment, or maybe a reverse gear or just a big button that said TAKE US BACK TO EARTH, didn't know that the server array also ran the air-making machinery and the food dispensary and everything that kept people alive.

I'm sure we had as many idiots as any other dumpround, but we made it just fine; that was all Sam, who ran the TC and kept the TC running the dumpround. The eighty-eight people on International Mars

Transport 2082/4/288 (which is what they called our dumpround; it was the 288th one fired off that April) all walked out of the dumpround on Mars carrying our complete, unlooted kits, and the militia that always stood by in case a dumpround landing involved hostages, arrests, or serious injuries didn't have a thing to do about us.

The five months in the dumpround were when I learned to read, and that has helped me so much—oh, hey, another box bumping up and down! Okay, botterogator, literacy as a positive value coming right up, all hot and ready for the new generation of Martians to suck inspiration from.

Hey, if you don't like irony, don't flash red lights at me, just edit it out. Yeah, authorize editing.

Anyway, with my info screen time, Sam made me do an hour of reading lessons for every two hours of games. Plus she coached me a lot. After a while the reading was more interesting than the games, and she was doing TC business so much of the time, and I didn't really have any other friends, so I just sat and worked on the reading. By the time we landed, I'd read four actual books, not just kid books I mean.

We came down on the parachute field at Olympic City, an overdignified name for what, in those long-ago days, was just two office buildings, a general store, and a nine-room hotel connected by pressurized tubes. The tiny pressurized facility was surrounded by a few thousand coffinsquats hooked into its pay air and power, and many thousand more running on their own fusion boxes. Olympica, to the south, was just a line of bluffs under a slope reaching way up into the sky.

It was the beginning of northern summer prospecting season. Sam towed me from lender to lender, coaching me on looking like a good bet to someone that would trust us with a share-deal on a prospecting gig. At the time I just thought rocks were, you know, rocks. No idea that some of them were ores, or that Mars was so poor in so many ores because it was dead tectonically.

So while she talked to bankers, private lenders, brokers, and plain old loan sharks, I dummied up and did my best to look like what she told them I was, a hard worker who would do what Sam told me. "Cap is quiet but he thinks, and we're a team."

She said that so often that after a while I believed it myself. Back at our coffinsquat every night, she'd make me do all the tutorials and read like crazy about rocks and ores. Now I can't remember how it was to not know something, like not being able to read, or recognize ore, or go through a balance sheet, or anything else I learned later.

Two days till we'd've gone into the labor pool and been shipped south to build roads and impoundments, and this CitiWells franchise broker, Hsieh Chi, called us back, and said we just felt lucky to him, and he had a quota to make, so what the hell.

Sam named our prospector gig the *Goodspeed* after something she'd read in a poem someplace, and we loaded up, got going, did what the software told us, and did okay that first summer around the North Pole, mostly.

Goodspeed was old and broke down continually, but Sam was a good directions-reader, and no matter how frustrating it got, I'd keep trying to do what she was reading to me—sometimes we both had to go to the dictionary, I mean who knew what a flange, a fairing, or a flashing was?—and sooner or later we'd get it figured out and roll again.

Yeah, botterogator, you can check that box for persistence in the face of adversity. Back then I'd've said I was just too dumb to quit if Sam didn't, and Sam was too stubborn.

Up there in the months and months of midnight sun, we found ore, and learned more and more about telling ore from not-ore. The gig's hopper filled up, gradually, from surface rock finds. Toward the end of that summer—it seemed so weird that Martian summers were twice as long as on Earth even after we read up about why—we even found an old volcanic vent and turned up some peridot, agate, amethyst, jasper, and garnet, along with three real honest-to-god impact diamonds that made us feel brilliant. By the time we got back from the summer prospecting, we were able to pay off Hsieh Chi's shares, with enough left over to buy the gig and put new treads on it. We could spare a little to rehab the cabin too; *Goodspeed* went from our dumpy old gig to our home, I guess. At least in Sam's mind. I wasn't so sure that home meant a lot to me.

Botterogator if you want me to inspire the new generation of Martians, you have to let me tell the truth. Sam cared about having a home, I didn't. You can flash your damn red light. It's true.

Anyway, while the fitters rebuilt *Goodspeed,* we stayed in a rented cabinsquat, sleeping in, reading, and eating food we didn't cook. We soaked in the hot tub at the Riebecker Olympic every single day—the only way Sam got warm. Up north, she had thought she was cold all the time because we were always working, she was small, and she just couldn't keep weight on no matter how much she ate, but even loafing around Olympic City, where the most vigorous thing we did was nap in the artificial sun room, or maybe lift a heavy spoon, she still didn't warm up.

We worried that she might have pneumonia or TB or something she'd brought from Earth, but the diagnostic machines found nothing unusual except being out of shape. But Sam had been doing so much hard physical work, her biceps and abs were like rocks, she was *strong*. So we gave up on the diagnosis machines, because that made no sense.

Nowadays everyone knows about Martian heart, but back then nobody knew that hearts atrophy and deposit more plaque in lower gravity, as the circulation slows down and the calcium that should be depositing into bones accumulates in the blood. Let alone that maybe a third of the human race have genes that make it happen so fast.

At the time, with no cases identified, it wasn't even a research subject; so many people got sick and died in the first couple decades of settlement, often in their first Martian year, and to the diagnostic machines it was all a job, ho hum, another day, another skinny nineteen-year-old dead of a heart attack. Besides, *all* the transportees, not just the ones that died, ate so much carb-and-fat food, because it was cheap. Why *wouldn't* there be more heart attacks? There were always more transportees coming, so put up another site about healthful eating for Mars, and find something else to worry about.

Checking the diagnosis machine was everything we could afford to do, anyway, but it seemed like only a small, annoying worry. After all, we'd done well, bought our own gig, were better geared up, knew more what we were doing. We set out with pretty high hopes.

Goodspeed was kind of a dumb name for a prospector's gig. At best it could make maybe 40 km/hr, which is not what you call roaring fast. Antarctic summer prospecting started with a long, dull drive down to Promethei Lingula, driving south out of northern autumn and into southern spring. The Interpolar Highway in those days was a gig track weaving southward across the shield from Olympic City to the Great Marineris Bridge. There was about 100 km of pavement, sort of, before and after the bridge, and then another gig track angling southeast to wrap around Hellas, where a lot of surface prospectors liked to work, and there was a fair bit of seasonal construction to be done on the city they were building in the western wall.

But we were going far south of Hellas. I asked Sam about that. "If you're cold all the time, why are we going all the way to the edge of the south polar cap? I mean, wouldn't it be nicer to maybe work the Bouches du Marineris or someplace near the equator, where you could stay a little warmer?"

"Cap, what's the temperature in here, in the gig cabin?"

"Twenty-two C," I said, "do you feel cold?"

"Yeah, I do, and that's my point," she said. I reached to adjust the temperature, and she stopped me. "What I mean is, that's room temperature, babe, and it's the same temperature it is in my suit, and in the fingers and toes of my suit, and everywhere. The cold isn't outside, and it doesn't matter whether it's the temperature of a warm day on Earth or there's CO_2 snow falling, the cold's in here, in me, ever since we came to Mars."

The drive was around 10,000 km as the road ran, but mostly it was pleasant, just making sure the gig stayed on the trail as we rolled past the huge volcanoes, the stunning view of Marineris from that hundred-mile-long bridge, and then all that ridge and peak country down south.

Mostly Sam slept while I drove. Often I rested a hand on her neck or forehead as she dozed in the co-driver's chair. Sometimes she shivered; I wondered if it was a long-running flu. I made her put on a mask and get extra oxygen, and that helped, but every few weeks I had to up her oxygen mix again.

All the way down I practiced pronouncing Promethei Lingula, especially after we rounded Hellas, because Sam looked a little sicker every week, and I was so afraid she'd need help and I wouldn't be able to make a distress call.

Sam figured Promethei Lingula was too far for most people—they'd rather pick through Hellas's or Argyre's crater walls, looking for chunks of something worthwhile thrown up from deep underground in those impacts, and of course the real gamblers always wanted to work Hellas because one big Hellas Diamond was five years' income.

Sam already knew what it would take me fifteen marsyears to learn: she believed in making a good bet that nobody else was making. Her idea was that a shallow valley like the Promethei Lingula in the Antarctic highlands might have more stuff swept down by the glaciers, and maybe even some of the kinds of exposed veins that really old mountains had on Earth.

As for what went wrong, well, nothing except our luck; nowadays I own three big veins down there. No, botterogator, I don't feel like telling you a damned thing about what I own, you're authorized to just look all that up. I don't see that owning stuff is inspiring. I want to talk about Sam.

We didn't find any veins, or much of anything else, that first southern summer. And meanwhile Sam's health deteriorated.

By the time we were into Promethei Lingula, I was fixing most meals and doing almost all the maintenance. After the first weeks I did all the exosuit work, because her suit couldn't seem to keep her warm, even on hundred percent oxygen. She wore gloves and extra socks even inside. She didn't move much, but her mind was as good as ever, and with her writing the search patterns and me going out and grabbing the rocks, we could still've been okay.

Except we needed to be as lucky as we'd been up in Boreas, and we just weren't.

Look here, botterogator, you can't make me say luck had nothing to do with it. Luck always has a shitload to do with it. Keep this quibbling up and just see if I inspire *any* new Martians.

Sometimes there'd be a whole day when there wasn't a rock that was worth tossing in the hopper, or I'd cover a hundred km of nothing but common basalts and granites. Sam thought her poor concentration made her write bad search patterns, but it wasn't that; it was plain bad luck.

Autumn came, and with it some dust storms and a sun that spiraled closer to the horizon every day, so that everything was dimmer. It was time to head north; we could sell the load, such as it was, at the depot at Hellas, but by the time we got to the Bouches de Marineris, it wouldn't cover more than a few weeks of prospecting. We might have to mortgage again; Hsieh Chi, unfortunately, was in the Vikingsburg pen for embezzling. "Maybe we could hustle someone, like we did him."

"Maybe *I* could, babe," Sam said. "You know the business a lot better, but you're still nobody's sales guy, Cap. We've got food enough for another four months out here, and we still have credit because we're working and we haven't had to report our hold weight. Lots of gigs stay out for extra time—some even overwinter—and nobody can tell whether that's because they're way behind like us, or they've found a major vein and they're exploiting it. So we can head back north, use up two months of supplies to get there, buy about a month of supplies with the cargo, go on short term credit only, and try to get lucky in one month. Or we can stay here right till we have just enough food to run for the Hellas depot, put in four months, and have four times the chance. If it don't work *Goodspeed*'ll be just as lost either way."

"It's going to get dark and cold," I pointed out. "Very dark and cold. And you're tired and cold all the time now."

"Dark and cold *outside the cabin*," she said. Her face had the stubborn set that meant this was going to be useless. "And maybe the dark'll make me eat more. All the perpetual daylight, maybe that's what's screwing my system up. We'll try the Bouches du Marineris next time, maybe those nice regular equatorial days'll get my internal clock working again. But for right now, let's stay here. Sure, it'll get darker, and the storms can get bad—"

"Bad as in we could get buried, pierced by a rock on the wind, maybe even flipped if the wind gets in under the hull," I pointed out. "Bad as in us and the sensors can only see what the spotlights can light. There's a reason why prospecting is a summer job."

She was quiet about that for so long I thought a miracle had happened and I'd won an argument.

Then she said, "Cap, I like it here in *Goodspeed*. It's home. It's ours. I know I'm sick, and all I can do these days is sleep, but I don't want to go to some hospital and have you only visit on your days off from a labor crew. *Goodspeed* is ours and I want to live here and try to keep it."

So I said yes.

For a while things got better. The first fall storms were water snow, not CO_2. I watched the weather reports and we were always buttoned up tight for every storm, screens out and treads sealed against the fine dust. In those brief weeks between midnight sun and endless night, when the sun rises and sets daily in the Promethei Lingula, the thin coat of snow and frost actually made the darker rocks stand out on the surface, and there were more good ones to find, too.

Sam was cold all the time; sometimes she'd cry with just wanting to be warm. She'd eat, when I stood over her and made her, but she had no appetite. I also knew how she thought: Food was the bottleneck. A fusion box supplied centuries of power to move, to compress and process the Martian air into breathability, to extract and purify water. But we couldn't grow food, and unlike spare parts or medical care we might need now and then, we needed food every day, so food would be the thing we ran out of first. (Except maybe luck, and we were already out of that). Since she didn't want the food anyway, she thought if she didn't eat we could stay out and give our luck more of a chance to turn.

The sun set for good; so far south, Phobos was below the horizon; cloud cover settled in to block the stars. It was darker than anywhere I'd ever been. We stayed.

There was more ore in the hold but not enough more. Still no vein. We had a little luck at the mouth of one dry wash with a couple tons of ore in small chunks, but it played out in less than three weeks.

Next place that looked at all worth trying was 140 km south, almost at the edge of the permanent cap, crazy and scary to try, but what the hell, everything about this was crazy and scary.

The sky had cleared for the first time in weeks when we arrived. With just a little CO_2 frost, it was easy to find rocks—the hot lights zapped the dry ice right off them. I found one nice big chunk of wolframite, the size of an old trunk, right off the bat, and then two smaller ones; somewhere up the glacial slopes from here, there was a vein, perhaps not under permanent ice. I started the analytic program mapping slopes and finds, and went out in the suit to see if I could find and mark more rocks.

Markeb, which I'd learned to pick out of the bunched triangles of the constellation Vela, was just about dead overhead; it's the south pole star on Mars. It had been a while since I'd seen the stars, and I'd learned more about what I was looking at. I picked out the Coal Sack, the Southern Cross, and the Magellanic Clouds easily, though honestly, on a clear night at the Martian south pole, that's like being able to find an elephant in a bathtub.

I went inside; the analysis program was saying that probably the wolframite had come from way up under the glacier, so no luck there, but also that there might be a fair amount of it lying out here in the alluvial fan, so at least we'd pick up something here. I stood up from the terminal; I'd fix dinner, then wake Sam, feed her, and tell her the semi-good news.

When I came in with the tray, Sam was curled up, shivering and crying. I made her eat all her soup and bread, and plugged her in to breathe straight body-temperature oxygen. When she was feeling better, or at least saying she was, I took her up into the bubble to look at the stars with the lights off. She seemed to enjoy that, especially that I could point to things and show them to her, because it meant I'd been studying and learning.

Yeah, botterogator, reinforce that learning leads to success. Sam'd like that.

"Cap," she said, "This is the worst it's been, babe. I don't think there's anything on Mars that can fix me. I just keep getting colder and weaker. I'm so sorry—"

"I'm starting for Hellas as soon as we get you wrapped up and have pure oxygen going into you in the bed. I'll drive as long as I can safely, then—"

"It won't make any difference. You'll never get me there, not alive," she said. "Babe, the onboard diagnostic kit isn't perfect but it's good enough to show I've got the heart of a ninety-year-old cardiac patient. And all the indicators have gotten worse in just the last hundred hours or so. Whatever I've got, it's killing me." She reached out and stroked my tear-soaked face. "Poor Cap. Make me two promises."

"I'll love you forever."

"I know. I don't need you to promise that. First promise, no matter where you end up, or doing what, you *learn*. Study whatever you can study, acquire whatever you can acquire, feed your mind, babe. That's the most important."

I nodded. I was crying pretty hard.

"The other one is kind of weird . . . well, it's silly."

"If it's for you, I'll do it. I promise."

She gasped, trying to pull in more oxygen than her lungs could hold. Her eyes were flowing too. "I'm scared to be buried out in the cold and the dark, and I can't *stand* the idea of freezing solid. So . . . don't bury me. Cremate me. I want to be *warm*."

"But you can't cremate a person on Mars," I protested. "There's not enough air to support a fire, and—"

"You promised," she said, and died.

I spent the next hour doing everything the first aid program said to do. When she was cold and stiff, I knew it had really happened.

I didn't care about *Goodspeed* anymore. I'd sell it at Hellas depot, buy passage to some city where I could work, start over. I didn't want to be in our home for weeks with Sam's body, but I didn't have the money to call in a mission to retrieve her, and anyway they'd just do the most economical thing—bury her right here, practically at the South Pole, in the icy night.

I curled up in my bunk and just cried for hours, then let myself fall asleep. That just made it worse; now that she was past rigor mortis she was soft to the touch, more like herself, and I couldn't stand to store her in the cold, either, not after what I had promised. I washed her, brushed her hair, put her in a body bag, and set her in one of the dry storage compartments with the door closed; maybe I'd think of something before she started to smell.

Driving north, I don't think I really wanted to live, myself. I stayed up too long, ate and drank too little, just wanting the journey to be over with. I remember I drove right through at least one bad storm at peak speed, more than enough to shatter a tread on a stone or to go into a sudden crevasse or destroy myself in all kinds of ways. For days in a row, in that endless black darkness, I woke up in the driver's chair after having fallen asleep while the deadman stopped the gig.

I didn't care. I wanted out of the dark.

About the fifth day, *Goodspeed*'s forward left steering tread went off a drop-off of three meters or so. The gig flipped over forward to the left, crashing onto its back. Force of habit had me strapped into the seat, and wearing my suit, the two things that the manuals the insurance company said were what you had to be doing any time the gig was moving if you didn't want to void your policy. Sam had made a big deal about that, too.

So after rolling, *Goodspeed* came to a stop on its back, and all the lights went out. When I finished screaming with rage and disappointment and everything else, there was still enough air (though I could feel it leaking) for me to be conscious.

I put on my helmet and turned on the headlamp.

I had a full capacitor charge on the suit, but *Goodspeed*'s fusion box had shut down. That meant seventeen hours of being alive unless I could replace it with another fusion box, but both the compartment where the two spare fusion boxes were stored, and the repair access to replace them, were on the top rear surface of the gig. I climbed outside, wincing at letting the last of the cabin air out, and poked around. The gig was resting on exactly the hatches I would have needed to open.

Seventeen—well, sixteen, now—hours. And one big promise to keep.

The air extractors on the gig had been running, as they always did, right up till the accident; the tanks were full of liquid oxygen. I could transfer it to my suit through the emergency valving, live for some days that way. There were enough suit rations to make it a real race between starvation and suffocation. The suit radio wasn't going to reach anywhere that could do me any good; for long distance it depended on a relay through the gig, and the relay's antenna was under the overturned gig.

Sam was dead. *Goodspeed* was dead. And for every practical purpose, so was I.

Neither *Goodspeed* nor I really needed that oxygen anymore, *but Sam does*, I realized. I could at least shift the tanks around, and I had the mining charges we used for breaking up big rocks.

I carried Sam's body into the oxygen storage, set her between two of the tanks, and hugged the body bag one more time. I don't know if I was afraid she'd look awful, or afraid she would look alive and asleep, but I was afraid to unzip the bag.

I set the timer on a mining charge, put that on top of her, and piled the rest of the charges on top. My little pile of bombs filled most of the space between the two oxygen tanks. Then I wrestled four more tanks to lie on the heap crosswise and stacked flammable stuff from the kitchen like flour, sugar, cornmeal, and jugs of cooking oil on top of those, to make sure the fire burned long and hot enough.

My watch said I still had five minutes till the timer went off.

I still don't know why I left the gig. I'd been planning to die there, cremated with Sam, but maybe I just wanted to see if I did the job right or something—as if I could try again, perhaps, if it didn't work? Whatever the reason, I bounded away to what seemed like a reasonable distance.

I looked up; the stars were out. I wept so hard I feared I would miss seeing them in the blur. They were so beautiful, and it had been so long.

Twenty kilograms of high explosive was enough energy to shatter all the LOX tanks and heat all the oxygen white hot. Organic stuff doesn't just burn in white-hot oxygen; it explodes and vaporizes, and besides fifty kilograms of Sam, I'd loaded in a good six hundred kilograms of other organics.

I figured all that out a long time later. In the first quarter second after the mining charge went off, things were happening pretty fast. A big piece of the observation bubble—smooth enough not to cut my suit and kill me, but hard enough to send me a couple meters into the air and backward by a good thirty meters—slapped me over and sent me rolling down the back side of the ridge on which I sat, smashed up badly and unconscious, but alive.

I think I dreamed about Sam, as I gradually came back to consciousness.

Now, look here, botterogator, of course I'd like to be able, for the sake of the new generation of Martians, to tell you I dreamed about her giving me earnest how-to-succeed advice, and that I made a vow there in dreamland to succeed and be worthy of her and all that. But in fact it was mostly just dreams of holding her and being held, and about laughing together. Sorry if that's not on the list.

The day came when I woke up and realized I'd seen the medic before. Not long after that I stayed awake long enough to say "hello." Eventually I learned that a survey satellite had picked up the exploding gig, and shot pictures because that bright light was unusual. An AI identified a shape in the dust as a human body lying outside, and dispatched an autorescue—a rocket with a people-grabbing arm. The autorescue flew out of Olympic City's launch pad on a ballistic trajectory, landed not far from me, crept over to my not-yet-out-of-air, not-yet-frozen body, grabbed me with a mechanical arm, and stuffed me into its hold. It took off again, flew to the hospital, and handed me over to the doctor.

Total cost of one autorescue mission, and two weeks in a human-contact hospital—which the insurance company refused to cover because I'd deliberately blown up the gig—was maybe twenty successful prospecting runs' worth. So as soon as I could move, they indentured me and, since I was in no shape to do grunt-and-strain stuff for a while, they found a little prospector's supply company that wanted a human manager for an office at the Hellas depot. I learned the job—it wasn't hard—and grew with the company, eventually as Mars's first indentured CEO.

I took other jobs, bookkeeping, supervising, cartography, anything where I could earn wages with which to pay off the indenture faster, especially jobs I could do online in my nominal hours off. At every job, because I'd promised Sam, I learned as much as I could. Eventually, a few days before my forty-third birthday, I paid off the indenture, quit all those jobs, and went into business for myself.

By that time I knew how the money moved, and for what, in practically every significant business on Mars. I'd had a lot of time to plan and think, too.

So that was it. I kept my word—oh, all right, botterogator, let's check that box too. Keeping promises is important to success. After all, here I am.

Sixty-two earthyears later, I know, because everyone does, that a drug that costs almost nothing, which everyone takes now, could have kept Sam alive. A little money a year, if anyone'd known, and Sam and me could've been celebrating anniversaries for decades, and we'd've been richer, with Sam's brains on the job too. And botterogator, you'd be talking to her, and probably learning more, too.

Or is that what I think now?

Remembering Sam, over the years, I've thought of five hundred things I could have done instead of what I did, and maybe I'd have succeeded as much with those too.

But the main question I think about is only—did she *mean* it? Did she see something in me that would make my bad start work out as well as it did? Was she just an idealistic smart girl playing house with the most cooperative boy she could find? Would she have wanted me to marry again and have children, did she intend me to get rich?

Every so often I regret that I didn't really fulfill that second promise, an irony I can appreciate now: she feared the icy grave, but since she burned to mostly water and carbon dioxide, on Mars she became mostly snow. And molecules are so small, and distribute so evenly, that whenever the snow falls, I know there's a little of her in it, sticking to my suit, piling on my helmet, coating me as I stand in the quiet and watch it come down.

Did she dream me into existence? I kept my promises, and they made me who I am . . . and was that what she wanted? If I am only the accidental whim of a smart teenage girl with romantic notions, what would I have been without the whim, the notions, or Sam?

Tell you what, botterogator, and you pass this on to the new generation of Martians: it's funny how one little promise, to someone or something a bit better than yourself, can turn into something as real as Samantha City, whose lights at night fill the crater that spreads out before me from my balcony all the way to the horizon.

Nowadays I have to walk for an hour, in the other direction out beyond the crater wall, till the false dawn of the city lights is gone, and I can walk till dawn or hunger turns me homeward again.

Botterogator, you can turn off the damn stupid flashing lights. That's all you're getting out of me. I'm going for a walk; it's snowing.

First published in

Life on Mars, edited by Jonathan Strahan, 2011.

ABOUT THE AUTHOR

John Barnes has thirty-one commercially published and two self-published novels, some of them to his credit, along with hundreds of magazine articles, short stories, blog posts, and encyclopedia articles. Most of his life he has written professionally, and for much of it he has been some kind of teacher, and in between he has held a large number of odd jobs involving math, show business, politics, and marketing, which have more in common than you'd think. He is married and lives in Denver.

Taught by the Moon:
Oral Traditions in Speculative Fiction
RHIANNON HELD

When drawing upon real archaeology to build a fictional world, it's perhaps no wonder that we often turn first to settled societies with written languages. Some of those societies have built impressive monuments and maintained complex governments—and left us a written record of those activities. It's easy to stop there and forget about mobile hunter-gatherer or tribal societies. Archaeology and ethnography have plenty to tell us about their history through oral traditions. And oral traditions have a lot to offer speculative fiction world-building.

First, a couple of definitions.

Ethnography is the study of living people and their culture, and is often used in conjunction with archaeological data to piece together the past. Ethnographers collect oral histories and oral traditions. Oral histories are first-hand accounts of past events or how the informant lived.

Oral traditions are composed of the stories passed down from one person to another that might also be called myths, fables, legends, or fairytales. When it comes to fiction, oral histories are already commonly used in speculative fiction world-building, whether it's a character reminiscing about how things were when she was a child, or one relating an important event that occurred only a few years before.

Oral traditions, on the other hand, are much less common to see in speculative fiction, despite the fact that they fit seamlessly into most of the subgenres. A traditional fantasy culture could be modeled on nomads or hunter-gatherers, rather than a settled society—but what about science fiction? Aliens could just as easily record their histories through oral traditions, if they have no written language. Cultures in a post-apocalyptic future could be forced to return to oral traditions as well, if writing has been lost. Or even if it hasn't been completely lost—without printing presses or the infrastructure to mass-produce a good paper substitute, word of mouth might well return as the best method of spreading news. Over the generations, news can grow into legends. Even urban fantasy beasties or monsters could have developed their own oral traditions, if they are sentient enough to have their own societies.

Not only do oral traditions fit naturally into speculative fiction, but they're incredibly useful, narratively speaking. The deep human impulse to participate in an oral tradition lurks in readers, quiescent because they were born into a culture with writing. Craft a fictional oral tradition correctly, and it *feels* real to readers because it taps into that impulse. Not only does it feel real, it feels *old*. Oral traditions don't arise overnight, so in modeling a fictional oral tradition after real ones, an author can take advantage of characteristics, some almost subliminal, that distinguish them from stories made up on the spot. A myth from an oral tradition can do more to make a reader subconsciously feel that a fictional culture is centuries old than pages of historical events.

Oral traditions can also reveal facts about a fictional culture, without having to lecture the readers through blatant exposition. Creation myths in particular are quite rich in opportunities to subtly present facts. The examples in this article are drawn from Northwest Coast and Columbia Plateau Native American tribes, but similar ones can be found all over the world.

In a story told in different versions by several Columbia Plateau tribes, Coyote made the first humans. In the time when animal people walked the earth, a giant beaver named Wishpoosh drowned anyone who tried to fish in his lake. The people asked Coyote for help, and he fought the monster long and hard, creating the valleys and lakes and twists and turns along the Columbia river as they grappled. Coyote realized he couldn't win, so he asked his three sisters who lived as berries in his stomach (that's another story) for advice, and they gave him a plan. Coyote changed into a fir branch, floated to the monster, and when it swallowed him, he hacked with his knife at the beaver's insides until it was dead. When he climbed out of the carcass, he cut it up, and from the pieces made the various tribes. As Coyote created each tribe he assigned them different temperaments and skills.

There's a lot going on there, all of which could be useful to build a fictional world. The story did not begin with blackness and nothingness— Wishpoosh and all the animals were already around before the tribes were made. A fictional culture presumably also arrived in an already-formed world, such as a science fiction culture crash-landing on a new planet, which you can reflect at the beginning of a myth.

This myth explains the geography that's most important to the people's lives—the Columbia River was central to the lives of Plateau tribes because they relied on it for food, through salmon. The myth shows how the people thought of themselves as interconnected, but with separate identities from tribes around them, formed from the same monster but different parts. And finally, the myth presents what people have constructed as their identifying characteristics. One presumes Coyote gave the best skills to the people telling the tale, but what's best? Bravery, or cleverness? Hunting, or fishing? The answer can reveal what attributes a fictional culture most prizes.

Another myth from across the Cascade Mountains illustrates this point. In this myth, with versions from around the Puget Sound, the Changer is born, kidnapped, and found as an adult by Blue Jay through a complicated set of circumstances too long to relate here. He starts on a journey home to return to his mother. Along the way, he encounters people doing all manner of foolish things. Some are using their heads instead of mauls (a kind of hammer) for woodworking. Others are allowing Raven to use living people instead of wood stakes lashed together to form his fish weir. The Changer shows them how to do things properly, and eventually makes it home to become the Moon.

Note the kind of skills the Changer is teaching: wood-working and fishing. He also teaches skills such as cooking in baskets and manufacturing arrows. All of these are key skills for daily life in Northwest cultures. In other versions of the myth, as the Changer encountered people he changed them into the first animals—for example, a man rowing with a paddle became Beaver, with the paddle for his tail. Similarly, the animals mentioned in the myth are the ones most important to daily life, whether they were hunted, or feared, or simply glimpsed everywhere. Turn that around, and you can show, without one explicit bit of exposition, just what's needed to survive in a fictional world, be it skills or knowledge of the environment.

Finally, myths can serve as excellent explanations. Why do salmon come up this tributary of the Columbia, but not the other? (Coyote's fault again.) Why is it so rainy west of the Cascade Mountains, but dry east of them? (Because the Ocean got angry and convinced the Great Spirit to raise the mountains when the people in the east tried to keep his children Clouds and Rain to themselves.) Turned to world-building purposes, explanation myths illustrate the great forces acting on a fictional culture. What floods, earthquakes, magic storms, or forgotten high technology weapons threaten them at impossible to predict intervals? What warm winds, fertile soils, or magical artifacts help them prosper through means they don't understand? Forces that can't be predicted, that can't be understood, need explanations.

Oral traditions are unfortunately linked with a couple tar pits of anthropological theory (one can thrash around for ages without getting anywhere in particular). Are similar mythological elements hardwired cross-culturally, or are they the coincidental results of happenstance? Or are similar elements signs of contact between two cultures, far in the past? In our world, those questions are incredibly frustrating to try to answer definitively, but the beauty of a fictional world with more than one culture is that you can decide the answer. Seed the same elements into the oral traditions of cultures that have been separate for centuries, and you've hinted at that ancient connection to the reader.

If anthropology theory doesn't interest you, on the other hand, there's also no need to lose yourself in attempting to learn all of the many possible abstract archetypes and themes. There are so many real world examples to feed one's creativity. Pick a culture, any culture, and model your fictional oral tradition on theirs, and the archetypes and themes will be already built in. It's best not to appropriate an oral tradition wholesale, but look at enough of them, and the bones start to become clear, allowing you to add a new skin on top.

Give the skin a wash and brush and you have a lovely fictional oral tradition, suitable for any speculative fiction subgenre. Smoothly, without direct exposition, it can tell your readers where the culture came from, what skills it values, and what forces and features in the environment shaped it. And beyond its narrative and expositional utility, it can serve to remind all of us of the place oral tradition once played—and still plays—in our lives, around the edges of our written words.

ABOUT THE AUTHOR

Rhiannon Held is the author of the urban fantasy Silver series from Tor, the latest novel of which is *Reflected*. She lives in Seattle, where she works as an archaeologist for an environmental compliance firm.

Dark Hearts & Brilliant Patches of Honor:
A Tribute to Manly Wade Wellman
JEREMY L. C. JONES

When Manly Wade Wellman died in 1986, he left behind a wealth of stories and novels that continue to resonate into the new century—the silver strings plucked by a master's hand.

"Manly was first and foremost a storyteller," said novelist David Drake, who was a friend of Wellman's and is now the owner of his literary estate.

Wellman did not ride trends. Instead, he plumbed the depths of American folk culture for the brightest metal and darkest coal.

"I think he deserves more attention [because of] both the incredible quality of his voice and his contributions to the genre's foundations," said James L. Sutter, who is both a novelist and the Managing Editor at Paizo Publishing. "It's important for us to recognize where modern fantasy comes from, and Wellman certainly had an impact on the field, even if (as I suspect) the average reader today has no idea who he is."

From his Appalachian-inspired fantasies of John the Balladeer to the sword and sorcery of Hok the Mighty and even the Wild West cavalry soldiers of the forgotten outpost of the soon-to-be reprinted *Fort Sun Dance*, Wellman remains readable and relevant to contemporary audiences. His characters stand tall and face the challenges presented to them; they do not cower or whine, as David Drake points out below.

"Wellman's folk tales of Silver John strike a universal chord that transcends category," said award-winning science fiction writer Mike Resnick, who wrote the introduction to the recent Paizo release of *Who Fears the Devil?*.

Furthermore, Wellman's work has that simultaneously familiar and strange, fresh and old, common and original quality of folktales and songs. It seems to be pulled from out collective past and shaped into something new and startling like traditional mountain music improvised on the spot.

"There is not a great deal of fantastic literature which draws mythic resonances from the American past," said editor and writer Darrell Schweitzer. "I think of some of Washington Irving and Stephen Vincent Benet and even some of Lovecraft, and then I am left grasping. The picture we have of a typical Wellman story is probably from *Who Fears the Devil?*, a sympathetic and intelligent treatment of a part of our country's past which most writers inevitably reduce to caricature."

Below, eight fans of Manly Wade Wellman's work—David Drake; John R. Fultz, fantasy novelist; Kenneth Hite, writer and game-designer; Samuel Montgomery-Blinn, editor and founder of the Manly Wade Wellman Award for Science Fiction and Fantasy; Mike Resnick; Darrell Schweitzer; James L. Sutter; and David Niall Wilson, novelist and founding CEO of Crossroads Press—talk about why Wellman's fiction endures, what they admire about it, and how it has influenced them.

What do you admire about Wellman's writing? And how has his writing influenced your own?

David Drake: I am continually delighted with Manly's quiet, folksy characters. I don't mean, "They speak in dialect," though in some cases they do; but generally his viewpoint is that of an intelligent, opinionated close observer. He doesn't attempt to be neutral, but he—the observer—will remain polite so long as the other party is polite. Manly's world is one in which courtesy is the default option—and would that the real world were more that way.

As for influence on me . . . well, not really. I was always a storyteller, not a stylist, myself. Watching—reading—Manly confirmed my predilection but didn't create it. Remember that Karl Wagner and I were Manly's friends and peers when we met, not students. Manly was incomparably more senior than we were, but we'd actually been selling fantasy more recently than Manly had. He got back into the field after we became friends.

The one exception to the "no influence" statement is *Old Nathan*. Those stories were started as conscious homage to Manly immediately after his death. Old Nathan isn't my version of John the Balladeer (Silver John if you must), but I was deliberately mining the same folk vein from which Manly had drawn his John stories.

John R. Fultz: Manly Wade Wellman's work combines the deep flavor of Appalachian folklore with horror and fantasy in a completely unique way. Being a native of Kentucky—born and raised in the Bluegrass State, I became a California transplant in '98—these stories have a special resonance for me. As a young fantasy fan and writer in Kentucky, it was strange to discover a fantasy writer who embraced his local culture and setting instead of replacing it with entirely fictional ones. I mean Robert E. Howard lived in Texas all his life, but most of his fantasies are set in fantastic worlds like The Hyborian Age and the Pre-Cataclysmic Age.

In Wellman's work, the sorcery, the magic, and even the horror, live and exist in the Mountains. His stories combine the best oral folktale traditions with the sensibilities of classic Weird Tales fiction. He found inspiration in actual Appalachian folklore, those enduring tales of haunted hollows, witches, devils, and nature magic.

His stories have a uniquely southern flair, in the best possible way, and they remain timeless pieces of weird fantasy/horror. John the Balladeer, or Silver John, as he's also called, is such an amazingly cool idea: A wandering minstrel with a silver-stringed guitar who travels the mountains battling ancient evils, dispelling curses, and generally ridding the world of supernatural wickedness. He's like Andy Griffith meets Gandalf.

Another great thing about these stories is the guitar itself, and the music John plays. I am also a guitar player, and the instrument plays a central role in a lot of "mountain culture"—as does music in general. I love how John's magic is tied up with his music, and sometimes that silver-stringed guitar can become a holy weapon in his hands. Devils beware!

As for how Wellman has influenced my own writing? Well, he makes me want to incorporate my own culture into my fantasy writing, something I've been playing with recently. Most specifically, I wrote a story called "The Gnomes of Carrick County," which follows a family of Irish immigrants coming into the Kentucky territory in about the year 1779, with a cameo by Daniel Boone himself. I really enjoyed this blending of actual history with fantasy, and I will come back to this in my work again.

Kenneth Hite: I think I most admire his devotion to taking the harder, but ultimately better, route into setting. He had to know the whole country before he showed it to us, and he knew just what to show us after he found it. Where Robert E. Howard, for example, delighted in making what we already knew seem fresh, Wellman provided chills, drilled deep wells of fantasy, from myths and folklore that we didn't already know. It's that combination of the wonderfully new and the age-old that all true fantasy aims for, and Wellman hit the gusher in West Virginia, not in Cimmeria or Mordor.

I don't write a lot of fiction, but Wellman's ability to find the strangeness and potential in American mythology has been a constant inspiration and lodestar in my nonfiction. "Suppressed Transmission" is essentially an attempt to prospect for productive wells across the worlds of folklore and fakelore alike. And by contrast, what Wellman could do with very familiar spirits indeed—with ghosts and Druids and Leonardo da Vinci—shows that nothing is over-used, it's just not been used correctly.

Samuel Montgomery-Blinn: Wellman had a marvelous ability to inhabit varied, colorful, vivid characters and (or perhaps exemplified) to write with dialect without stumbling into an unreadable, stumbling mess. A very close second is his limitless stamina in producing so much work in so many genres for such a long time. He's nonetheless influenced me in how I read short fiction and in kindling an interest in reading in varied genres and in developing a folklorist's nose and appreciation for North Carolina writing.

Mike Resnick: I admire the feel of authenticity. I know these are original stories, not folk tales from the 19th Century, but they have an authentic *feel* about them, which means that a) Wellman was an artist, and b) he did his homework.

By graduating from the pulps to the kind of stories we remember him for, he showed that one could improve, and that you needn't be a bottom-dweller forever. I began my career with Burroughs and Howard pastiches; Manly showed me, by example, that I could write my own stuff and make a living from it.

Darrell Schweitzer: I can't say he has deeply influenced my own work. I do admire the way his first person narrators (like John) have an authentic narrative voice, and therefore present the fantastic as if it is part of life that is actually lived. It doesn't feel made-up.

James L. Sutter: It's his voice and sense of place. As soon as I read the first few sentences of "John's My Name," I was hooked. After reading through all the Silver John short stories, I felt not just like I'd been entertained, but that I'd learned something as well. Reading those stories gives you a feel for a very particular time and place in American history, both through the writing and through the uniquely southern mythology and superstitions he presents. How you boil down a people and a place to that sort of snapshot is beyond me, but I think it all starts in the voice—he's not afraid to ride the fine line between authenticity and alienating the reader, and so far I've yet to see him fall. But I definitely come away from his work wanting to write in voices other than my own.

David Niall Wilson: I love the way he could bring the mountains of North Carolina to life. He peopled them with the ordinary, and the extraordinary—characters of great wisdom and power, dark, evil hearts, and brilliant patches of honesty and honor. He wrote modern fairy tales, and helped to keep the legends and folklore of our country intact.

Which genre(s) do you think Wellman did the best, and why?

David Drake: A couple of Manly's mainstream novels of the '50s—in particular *Candle of the Wicked*—are to my mind his best writing. That said, his early John the Balladeer stories are wonderful and unique; a strain of particularly American fantasy writing which has never been equaled.

His Young Adult novels are very good of their type, but they don't attempt to rise above it.

His SF is handicapped by the fact that he didn't understand science; his storytelling ability will often carry the reader nonetheless.

His earlier fantasies, many of them published in *Weird Tales* in the '30s and '40s, are very solid performers in the field but rarely rise much above it. Again, because he was such a good storyteller, these fantasies are regularly reprinted.

His non-fiction is well researched but here—to a degree I don't see in his fiction—his adoration for Thomas Wolfe comes to the fore in a pretentious, inflated, fashion. I myself have difficulty piercing the style to get to the content.

John R. Fultz: I'm not as widely-read in Wellman as some. I'm mainly a Silver John fan. So that's my favorite because these tales really "sing" for me (pun intended). Silver John is such a rarity in literature: A southerner who is not confined to some insulting archetype, who is not a font of ignorance and backward attitudes, but who carries a vast store of occult knowledge. A hero for the mountain folk, and a true American icon of weird fantasy.

Just the idea of a traveling, guitar-playing wizard who knows the secrets of the ancient land is enough to get me interested. And when you read the actual tales, you feel the presence of a master storyteller at work.

Kenneth Hite: I haven't remotely read enough Wellman to know the answer to that. He wrote a prodigious amount of history I haven't read, for one thing. But I do know that his fantastic horror is some of the finest anyone has ever produced, while his science fiction is mostly just pretty good. But even then, his Thirtieth Century yarns can easily compare with Piper or Blish or even lesser Jack Vance.

Why is his fantastic horror so good? I think, again, it's because of his mastery of setting. In their own ways, Lovecraft and King have demonstrated that horror that truly gets inside you has to start in a place, a place that's as real as possible. Poe can transcend that requirement; so can Ligotti. But most horrorists aren't Poe or Ligotti.

Samuel Montgomery-Blinn: If I can cheat, I'll pick: short fiction. His historical, non-fiction, crime, mystery, science fiction, and fantasy novels and comic scripts do indeed spread out backwards and into the cosmos(es), but he was also able to tell a great many great stories in a handful of pages and that's a rare thing.

Mike Resnick: I confess to only reading his fantasy and science fiction, but when I did the intro to the recent reprint of *Who Fears the Devil?* I learned, while researching him, that he was nominated for a Pulitzer for his history, so I'd have to think he probably did that as well as his Silver John stories.

Darrell Schweitzer: And I have not read all of them. He wrote a lot of historical fiction, and historical fiction for younger readers (a series about the Civil War, from the Southern viewpoint) which have not survived, not because they are not as good, but because, particularly in the US, most readers aren't much interested in history. Fantasy survives better. That is where the market for Wellman fiction is.

The one piece of his science fiction which has had considerable longevity is *Twice in Time,* although I have recommended this book to people and gotten back the response, "I didn't know Wellman ever wrote science fiction." Yes, he did, but mostly for a short period. He allegedly had a falling out with John W. Campbell over that one. Campbell wanted to meddle, Manly said no, and he sold it to *Startling Stories* instead, where it appeared in the March 1940 issue.

I cannot imagine, though, that Campbell could have published *Twice in Time* at this time, though, because it is too similar to de Camp's *Lest Darkness Fall* (Unknown December, 1939). The difference is that in the Wellman version, the man from our present becomes a famous person in our own past, while in de Camp's he does not, and branches off into an alternate history. But both books have many of the same virtues.

So the honest answer is that I cannot really say in which genre Manly wrote best. I have never read his mystery fiction, for instance. Did you know he once beat out William Faulkner in a story contest in *Ellery Queen's Mystery Magazine*? All I can tell you is that the fantasy has survived better, and that may be as much a result of the market and of American culture is it is a reflection of the excellence of Manly's fantasy vs. his work in other genres.

James L. Sutter: My experience is primarily with his Silver John material, which I'd classify as somewhere between fantasy and Americana, and I feel like the latter aspect must give it an edge (it's like a whole class in Appalachian folklore!). But I look forward to reading further, and potentially being proven wrong!

David Niall Wilson: His magical fantasies are my personal favorites. I know he wrote a lot of science fiction, but it never hit me the way his folklore-based fantasy did. I also love his young adult novels. Though formulaic, he has way of telling a story that engages the minds of young readers, even though the settings and characters are from our past.

In whom do you see yourself, Silver John, Hok the Mighty, or another of Wellman's characters?

David Drake: Good God Almighty! I don't see myself in any of Manly's characters. Manly and I have organized our lives—certainly our working lives—in remarkably similar ways, but we are/were different men.

Though . . . Manly's heroes always faced problems instead of whining or running, just as Manly himself did. I try to be that sort of man myself.

John R. Fultz: Oh, definitely Silver John. I've made magic on my guitar for decades, but I wish I could cast the kinds of spells that ring out from John's silver strings.

Kenneth Hite: On my very best days, I'm a knockoff of John Thunstone. Occultist, layabout, *bon vivant,* and always up for stabbing a werewolf. But Wellman's characters by and large seem almost prodigiously good-hearted and self-possessed; even Thunstone seems like he's just pretending to be a playboy. Like Batman.

Samuel Montgomery-Blinn: In the end it's John the Balladeer. I'm an Indiana farmer's son, and looking around my office I see a guitar, scattered singer-songwriter sheet music, and a great many books. If only I had any of the talent or magic or half the brains and courage and heart . . .

Mike Resnick: I see myself doing what Manly did—telling the tales of more interesting characters than myself. Probably not the answer you're looking for, but it's an honest one.

Darrell Schweitzer: I suppose all artistic types may fancy a little of themselves in John the Balladeer—*not* "Silver John"—but to be honest, no, I do not identify with any of Manly's characters.

James L. Sutter: As a musician myself, it's hard not to love Silver John. Even though fantasy RPGs have had the "bard" class for a long time, it's still rare to see someone take the magical musician idea and really make it work. John's a shaman with a guitar, exorcising spirits with his silver strings. What more can you ask for?

David Niall Wilson: I've won awards for poetry, and I've played guitar for over thirty years. I love the idea of Silver John—his integrity, his courage. I am not Silver John, of course, but he is the man I would be if had that magic . . . Music is like that, and I've written a lot about musicians myself—and about North Carolina, for that matter. So I will say that Silver John is the character I identify with . . .

Why has Manly Wade Wellman's fiction endured?

John R. Fultz: I suppose there are two reasons. One, because of Wellman's superb imagination, his sheer storytelling skill, and the iconic nature of his creations. Two, because writers and editors over the decades have made sure that people don't forget Manly Wade Wellman. Various editions of his Silver John stories have been assembled, most recently the Planet Stories collection of *Who Fears the Devil?*

My own treasured, time-worn copy of Wellman tales is called *John the Balladeer* and it was published by Baen back in 1988. I'm so glad Planet has repackaged these stories for a modern audience—and they've given it a terrific new cover painting. The one I have features a Steve Hickman painting of John playing guitar by the fireside while a bat-winged succubus looks over his shoulder. My '88 edition also has a nice foreword by the great David Drake. David is certainly one of the reasons the Wellman stories have not been forgotten.

Kenneth Hite: Plain and simply—because it's vastly better than that of his peers. His stories are gripping without being overly melodramatic; his settings are lively without overwhelming the tale; his characters are heroic and human. And his prose, the rhythm and the words of it, simply work. Even his most formulaic stories manage to pose some interesting problem, or present an arresting event, on their way to the conclusion. All that keeps Wellman's work alive and interesting where Nictzyn Dyalhis or even Seabury Quinn are mere historical curiosities.

Samuel Montgomery-Blinn: Wellman wrote well and sharply, widely and prolifically, in short fiction and at length, and did so at a time (and for a long time) when his work could pick up from those who had come before (particularly Edgar Rice Burroughs) and form a core part of the emerging canon of the emerging genres.

Also, with his stomping grounds in North Carolina and its surrounds being such fertile ground for writers and readers, he was able to directly influence a generation of writers in those genres and lengths; those students, fans, and friends would go on to write directly (e.g. Dave Drake's *Old Nathan,* Mike Mignola's *The Crooked Man*) and indirectly (Warren Rochelle, Andy Duncan, C.S. Fuqua) influenced fiction, and so on, and here we are still talking about Wellman and his stories and will likely be for many years to come.

At some point, a writer's body of work becomes a self-fulfilling force for its own endurance—I know more about Wellman's work through the shadows it casts than from direct contact with the source material.

Darrell Schweitzer: It's not enough to say "because it was good," since any number of good writers have fallen into oblivion. That he was associated with *Weird Tales* in its great age is not the answer either, because more and more readers of his work have never laid eyes on a copy of *WT* from the '30s. The answer has to be that it retains his charm, and that it still fills a need. I think the great strength of his work (other than its technical excellence) is that it is distinctly American, his John the Balladeer and John Thunstone stuff at least.

Incidentally, it is always "John the Balladeer" and never "Silver John." This latter appellation was invented by the publisher, and Manly did not approve of it. Also, one never uses the term "hillbilly." Manly explained to me that if you go up in the hills and use that term, the hearer may feel "it is his bound duty to remove your neck from your body." Unsurprisingly, then, he did not much care for the film *The Legend of Hillbilly John* and congratulated me on not having seen it.

The best of Wellman's fiction of this sort is literate, elegant, and authentic where very little else by other writers is. I tell you this as a former editor of Weird Tales, who has seen plenty of fake hillbilly stuff in the slushpile, always from people who do not live in, and I suspect have never even visited, the Southern Appalachian area.

James L. Sutter: Unfortunately, I don't think [Wellman's fiction] has endured in the public eye—or rather, nowhere near as well as it deserves. I know that before I started working on Planet Stories, I had never heard of him before, which is a bit mind-boggling considering how many awards he's won and how many popular authors cite him as an influence.

David Niall Wilson: It has endured with fans of his work because it is sincere and simple, at once magical and very believable. Silver John, as an example, is the man we all wish we could be, the hero, but not in a Superman sense—in a real sense. Manly wrote a lot of different things in a lot of different genres. His young adult novels are amazingly accessible, and his work in comics has lingered—though not so many are aware of it.

For instance, I wonder how many know that—when asked to recreate Superman for a rival comic book company, he created Captain Marvel—and when he wrote the first script, he managed to use the letters of his name as the first letters in the words in a way he could come back to it in court, if asked, and *prove* that he created it. He was an amazingly talented man.

ABOUT THE AUTHOR

Jeremy L. C. Jones is a freelance writer, editor, and teacher. He is the Staff Interviewer for *Clarkesworld Magazine* and a frequent contributor to *Kobold Quarterly* and *Booklifenow.com*. He teaches at Wofford College and Montessori Academy in Spartanburg, SC. He is also the director of Shared Worlds, a creative writing and world-building camp for teenagers that he and Jeff VanderMeer designed in 2006. Jones lives in Upstate South Carolina with his wife, daughter, and flying poodle.

Another Word: Debts

DANIEL ABRAHAM

There are only a few books that I reread. Walter Tevis' *The Queen's Gambit,* some of Dorothy Sayers' Lord Peter Wimsey mysteries, Camus' *The Plague,* and a few others. They've become like having coffee with an old friend or watching *Casablanca* again; a place of comfort and familiarity. A way to reconnect with part of my past. And sometimes—more often than I expect really—a place to discover something new about how I read and how I write.

A few weeks ago, I started in on Dorothy Dunnett's House of Niccolo series for what I think will be the fourth time. It's my bedtime reading, so I only do a few pages a day and a chapter at most. I've just gotten to the three-quarter mark on *The Spring of the Ram,* second book of eight, and what I'm discovering this time through is how much of it stuck with me the last times I read it, and how much of an effect it's had on me.

There are some ways I knew that Dunnett had become one of my influences. She writes about economics and trade in the 1400s, and was passionate enough about it that I read a few books about medieval and renaissance banking, which served as one of the basic conceits in my Dagger and Coin books. But there are other things all through it that I didn't know I was using, adopting, changing. In the first part of *Spring of the Ram,* for instance, there is a brief incident in which the company doctor receives a rare book about optics and the structure of the eye. In my novel, *The Price of Spring,* a physician studies a rare book on optics and the structure of the eye as one of the critical moments in the plot. I didn't remember the Dunnett scene when I plotted out the novel, and the function of the two physicians and their books in the stories is utterly different. But it was a detail of such weird specificity, it reminded me of the debt I owe to those books.

The flow of ideas and techniques in fiction—or painting, or dance, or any art really—is fraught and contentious. Mostly that's because of the (very legitimate) specter of plagiarism. There are a lot of examples of people taking other people's complete works, filing off the serial numbers and claiming to have come up with them on their own. Shia LaBeouf lifting dialog, story, and structure from Daniel Clowes and then "apologizing" with unattributed quotations from other apologies by other people. Rand Paul lifting passages from Wikipedia and movies. The poet Christian Ward making only minor changes the works of at least half a dozen other poets and passing the poems off as his own. The appropriations and dishonesty of people like that does a disservice to more than the writers whose works they stole. It also puts a stigma on the conversation about the ways in which artists and writers legitimately borrow and reinterpret and take inspiration from each other.

Austin Kleon's brilliant little book *Steal Like an Artist* is about, among other things, the division between plagiarism and inspiration, between studying other artists to do your own work and making a claim on the work that they've done. Kameron Hurley's recent essay about her own debt to the traditions of violent, hypermasculine protagonists as a basic building block in her own work and the transformations that came from that choice is an example. Hurley is very aware of what she's borrowed, how she's used it, and how those changes made something genuinely and profoundly original.

And that, of course, is the trick.

Anyone who becomes an artist—writer, painter, dancer—had a first experience of their art as it was done by someone else. We've built up a lifetime of experience not only as performers but first as audience. We've learned from Ursula Le Guin what a good sentence looks like, and from Hemingway that there's more than one kind of good sentence. We've learned from Shakespeare and Raymond Chandler how to turn a phrase. The exercises new authors do in order to learn—retype a page of your favorite author's work, start with a paragraph from a published book and then write your own continuation, create a passage in the voice of an author you admire—are ways to internalize the choices and insights of the people who came before us. That's what the process is.

We build a library of experience from it. The toolbox we work with is made up from bits and pieces of other writers, other stories. We make the world by experience and mimicry, by faking it until we find ourselves growing into our own idiosyncratic styles. The toolbox we have can only be made from the experiences we put into it, and for writers, many of those experiences are the ones we had reading other people's books. What I have in the back of my mind depends on what I put in there. My sense of what the fourth act of a play *does* comes from studying Shakespeare and reading Robertson Davies. My distaste for explicit violence grows from (or at least through) my failure to enjoy Thomas Harris. The idea of the magical being Clarity-of-Sight, also called Blindness that figured so much in my book had its seeds in Tobias Beventini's awe at being given a book on optics by Dorothy Dunnett. What comes out of us draws on what we've put into ourselves. Where else could it come from?

And that's just true of writers and artists. That's everyone.

Which is how I came to think about a different kind of debt.

My daughter is in grade school now, and part of what I see, watching her grow up, is how much she relies on what she's heard and seen. I hear her use phrases the way I do, or my wife does. I see how her school's policies on discipline come back out from her. She's just like me this way, creating herself out of bits and pieces of what's around her. And some of the people she's learning from, who she's basing herself on, are fictional. She has opinions about Aang and Katara from the "Avatar: The Last Airbender" TV series on Nickelodeon. We also had a long conversation not long ago about why Betty and Veronica need to stop treating Archie like a prize to be fought over. She cares deeply what happens to September during her journeys in Fairyland and dressed as the Marquess for Halloween.

I've never been in favor of censorship for kids. The rule in my house is that she can read anything she wants, so long as she's willing to talk about it afterward. My stance on movies is tougher, but her tastes are tamer even than mine for her so it doesn't really come up. But as a writer—as one of the folks who's putting things out there for other people to fold into the back of their minds—this all has given me pause.

A debt means something is owed, and I am coming to suspect that I may owe something to whoever gives me their time and attention. The stories I tell, even if they're consciously forgotten, are in their heads now. The scenes and people and actions I ask them to imagine are part of their experience. For me, a book on optics can rise to the surface with its origins unrecognized. For my daughter, a turn of phrase can come out of her mouth without her being at all aware that she's quoting her mother or her teacher or me. That's what it is to be a pattern-matching device fitted with will and desire. That's what it is to be human.

I spend my life trying to put things into people's minds, trying to give them bits of information and experience that mean enough to them that they remember my stories. Maybe even, without knowing, incorporate them into their own. There are consequences to that, even if I never see them.

I'm still struggling with the nature of the debt that fact incurs. Should I only ever be upbeat and positive? Should I never show someone being mean or glib or dismissive? Should I censor what I do so that what I leave with my readers has a better chance of helping them find a gentle phrase when the hard times come? I can't quite believe that. My ambivalence about fiction as an engine of morality is already on record, but at the very least, we owe the people we write for, the people who see our paintings or attend our dances or who we raise into adults, the effort of remembering that we're all made from pieces of other people. What we put out there is going to come back.

And probably not in the way we predict.

ABOUT THE AUTHOR

Daniel Abraham is a writer of genre fiction with a dozen books in print and over thirty published short stories. His work has been nominated for the Nebula, World Fantasy, and Hugo Awards and has been awarded the International Horror Guild Award. He also writes as MLN Hanover and (with Ty Franck) as James S. A. Corey. He lives in the American Southwest.

Editor's Desk:
Support Jay Lake
NEIL CLARKE

Over the years, I've taken advantage of these editorials to point out worthy causes and the good that our community has done. I've had the opportunity to talk about things that have ranged from crowdfunding projects by some of our authors to the amazing support my family and I received after my heart attack. These are stories that need to be told. Some are long and protracted. Others, like this one, are short and pointed calls to action.

My first exposure to Jay Lake was through his short fiction. Out of nowhere, his stories were suddenly appearing in every magazine I read. To be prolific and talented is a rare gift. Soon after, I started reading his blog, then his novels, and even had the opportunity to publish a few of his stories in *Clarkesworld*. He supported us from the beginning and that trust will always be remembered. Despite that fact that we live on opposite sides of the country, I've had the pleasure of meeting him several times, most recently at Worldcon. I think it only took five minutes to seal my high opinion of him.

Jay is also a father and a terminal cancer patient. The full story of Jay's lengthy battle with cancer can be found on his blog. (jlake.com/blog) It's a devastatingly heartbreaking story, even if you don't know him.

Most recently, Jay volunteered to take part in an NIH trial. Basically he has become a guinea pig for new and untested treatments in the hope of extending his life and having more time with friends and family.

Unfortunately, the NIH doesn't cover all the expenses and insurance companies won't help pay for trials. As you can imagine, the expenses involved multiply quickly and surpass even the most well-planned budget.

Thanks to YouCaring.com, Shlomi Harif was able to set up a way to channel donations to Jay. The initial goal was set to $15,000 and the good news is that amount has already been raised by thanks to the generous contributions of many in and outside our community.

The campaign ends in early February and there is still time to make sure Jay has a financial safety net for those surprise expenses that have already begun to mount.

To participate, visit:

http://tinyurl.com/jay-lake-fundraiser

Please support Jay if you can. If nothing else, keep him and his loved ones in your thoughts and join us in wishing them the best.

ABOUT THE AUTHOR

Neil Clarke is the editor of *Clarkesworld Magazine,* owner of Wyrm Publishing and a two-time Hugo Nominee for Best Editor (short form). He currently lives in NJ with his wife and two children.

Cover Art:
Space Sirens

JULIE DILLON

Julie Dillon is a freelance illustrator working in Northern California. She creates science fiction and fantasy artwork for books, magazines and games. Julie was a 2013 Hugo Award Nominee for Best Artist.

WEBSITE

www.jdillon.net